HIDING OUT

Elizabeth Gail

Gail 11

HIDING
OUT

HILDA STAHL

Tyndale House Publishers, Inc.
Wheaton, Illinois

Visit the exciting Web site for kids at www.cool2read.com and the
Elizabeth Gail Web site at www.elizabethgail.com

Formerly titled *Elizabeth Gail and the Frightened Runaways*

Designed by Beth Sparkman

ISBN 0-8423-4074-2, mass paper

Printed in the United States of America

09 08 07 06 05 04 03 02
10   9   8   7   6   5   4   3   2   1

Dedicated with love to
Kay, Tammy, Shauna,
Melody, and Andrea

CONTENTS

❀ ❀ ❀

1. A Noise in the Barn. 1

2. Piano Lesson 9

3. A Big Decision. 17

4. Trouble 25

5. More Pain 33

6. Snoopy Susan 45

7. Ms. Kremeen 55

8. Double Trouble 67

9. Tattletale Toby 79

10. Discovery 89

11. A Talk in the Study 99

12. April and May 109

13. Morris and Evelyn Stern 119

14. Help 127

A Noise in the Barn

LIBBY gripped the wire handle of the red plastic bucket of grain as she slowly turned away from Snowball's stall. Had she heard a sneeze? First her heart seemed to stand still, then almost leap through her jacket. Would her real mother dare to sneak up on her and kidnap her so the Johnsons couldn't adopt her?

Snowball nickered and pawed the dirt floor of her stall. A barn cat mewed. Libby held her breath and cocked her head, listening intently. What was wrong with her? She had no reason to fear. Mother had signed the papers saying the Johnson family could adopt her. Mother had said she would never bother Libby or the Johnson family again.

Slowly, painfully, Libby released her breath and turned back to Snowball's stall. "I shouldn't be so jumpy, Snowball," Libby said as she poured the grain into the white filly's feed container. "Dad said we have nothing to fear. He said everything was going to be all right. I believe him, Snowball. He loves me! All the Johnson family love me even if I am only a welfare kid."

Libby rubbed her hand down Snowball's neck. "They won't change their minds, Snowball. I know they won't!" She hesitated and tried to stop the shiver that ran up and down her spine. "Will they? I just wish I could be good all the time! Then I wouldn't have anything to worry about."

Snowball lifted her head and nuzzled Libby's shoulder. "I love you, Snowball. I'm glad you belong to me."

With a smile Libby pushed her short brown hair out of her face and walked out of the stall. Suddenly she stopped, her hazel eyes wide. That had not been a cat sneezing! Someone was in the barn! Ben, Susan, Kevin, and Toby were all in the house watching Saturday morning cartoons. Chuck was in town at his store, and Vera was getting ready to go to town.

Who was in the barn? Should she run to the house to get Ben? He was always brave. She dare not stay out much longer. Vera would be waiting to take her to her piano lesson with Rachael Avery. And she would not miss her piano lesson!

"Who's in here?" Libby's voice sounded weak and scared. She'd meant it to come out loud and demanding. She cleared her throat and tried again. Oh, what if it were Mother?

With her back pressed against Snowball's stall door, Libby looked around. Whoever was in the barn had to be hiding in one of the stalls. Or had she just imagined the sneeze because she was worried about Mother taking her?

She forced her legs to support her as she slowly walked down the concrete aisle of the barn. She stopped, her heart racing wildly, and stared at a stack of baled hay. Someone could be behind the hay. She had hidden there just last night when they'd played hide-and-seek after school. Kevin had finally given up and called her free.

Slowly Libby walked around the bales of hay and peeked down into her favorite hiding spot. She jumped back in surprise. Someone was hiding there! But it wasn't Mother.

Libby wanted to run away screaming, but

3

she stood beside the hay and forced her body to stop shaking. "I see you! I see you in the hay. Come out right now!" She waited, poised for flight.

A girl just a little taller than Libby slowly crept from the hiding place and stood up. She had light brown hair and brown eyes. She stared at Libby as she rubbed her hands down her jeans, then stuffed them into the pockets of her green jacket. "Hi, Libby," she said in a small voice.

"April?" Libby whispered in surprise, stepping back until she bumped against the wall. "April Brakie?"

The girl shook her head. "No. I'm May. April's over there."

Libby jerked her head around to see an identical-looking girl on the other side of the hay.

"Hi, Libby." April grinned sheepishly as she walked around the hay and stopped beside Libby. "Are you mad?"

Libby stared at the twins, then slowly shook her head. "What are you doing here?"

"We came to find you," said May urgently. "We need help."

"We heard you're going to be adopted," said April.

"We said if Elizabeth Gail Dobbs can find herself a family, then maybe we can too."

"You mean you ran away again?" Libby stared at the girls, remembering the first time she'd seen them. All three of them had lived with the Mason family for about four months. April and May looked so much alike and had dressed exactly alike so that no one could tell them apart. Mrs. Mason had beat them both for any wrongdoing in order to make sure that the offender had been punished.

April sneezed, then wiped the back of her hand across her nose. She looked pale and too thin, thinner than May. "We had to get away, Libby. We couldn't stay there."

"We heard Mrs. Blevins talking about you," said May with a giggle. "She said a wonderful family was adopting you. We said if Libby can do it, we can too. We came to meet your family and see if they'd take us."

"Oh! Oh, dear!" Libby shook her head. "I don't know. I don't know what they'd say if they knew you had run away. Who were you living with?" She saw the hard look on April's face and the fear in May's eyes. "Tell me, girls."

April nervously pushed her long brown hair

back from her thin pale face. "Remember Morris and Evelyn Stern?"

Libby's stomach tightened into a hard knot, and the barn seemed to spin. "No, I don't remember them."

"Yes you do, Elizabeth Gail Dobbs!" cried May, catching Libby's icy hand in hers and squeezing it. "You remember living with them."

"No!" She pushed the memory back and would not let it out. "No!"

April shrugged. "If that's the way you want it, then that's the way it'll be."

"You must remember, Libby," cried May in alarm. "Then you'll know how much we need you to help us or hide us or something! We can't go back to them! We can't!"

Libby jerked free and turned to run from the barn, but May grabbed her again and knocked her into the corner of the stall, where she struck her arm. Pain shot through her and she cried out.

"Don't hurt her, May," said April sharply. "She'll help us. I know she will."

"Will you, Libby?" May's voice was low and soft and pleading, and Libby wanted to shout no! "Please, Libby."

Slowly Libby stood up, holding her throbbing right arm protectively. "I'll think about it. I have to go to town right now. When I get back, I'll tell you my answer."

May's thin hand reached out pleadingly. "You won't tell on us, will you?"

Libby shook her head, glad that she could help erase the fear from May's eyes. "I promise not to tell. You girls stay hidden in here. I'll be home by noon, and I'll bring you something to eat."

"Thanks, Libby," said April, wrapping her arms around herself and hunching her thin shoulders. Pieces of hay clung to her hair. Dark circles around her eyes made them look large in her pale face.

Libby wanted to take both girls into the house and ask Vera to mother them and give them a home forever. Finally she turned away and walked out of the barn into the cool September air.

She lifted her pointed chin and squared her shoulders. Goosy Poosy honked from the chicken pen. Rex barked a short, sharp bark and ran to Libby's side. She rested her hand on his head, then cried out in pain. Gingerly she rubbed her arm.

Determinedly she ran to the back door of the house. She would not think about her arm

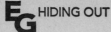

or the Brakie twins right now. She had to go to her piano lesson with Rachael Avery.

She opened the door and stepped inside, leaning weakly against the closed door. She would *not* remember Morris and Evelyn Stern!

Piano Lesson

LIBBY tried to ignore the pain in her arm as she followed Rachael Avery into the music room. The baby grand piano gleamed brightly where the sun shone onto it through a window.

"I hate to see winter come," said Rachael with a smile as she waited for Libby to stand her books on the piano and take off her jacket. "I'd like to see fall last until spring," Rachael commented, her long black hair flowing down her back and over her slender shoulders. Several pictures in the grouping on the wall beside the piano showed her in concert. Libby had often stared at the pictures, pretending she was in concert instead of the famous Rachael Avery.

Libby bit back a moan as she hung her jacket on a wooden hall tree next to the door. When Vera had asked her why she was pale, she'd answered that she was excited about the lesson. Once she started playing, her arm would stop hurting.

"Did you practice your hour a day this week, Elizabeth?" Rachael sat on her stool beside the piano and smiled at Libby.

Libby nodded. "I had a little trouble but Mom helped me." Libby sat on the bench and opened the first book. A groan escaped when she moved her arm, and Rachael asked if anything was wrong. Libby quickly explained that it was nothing, maybe a little cramp.

"I heard Mrs. Johnson play in church last Sunday. I was visiting your church with my husband's sister. Mrs. Johnson is very talented," said Rachael.

Libby flushed with pleasure. "I want to play as well as she does."

"You will—and better." Rachael patted Libby's shoulder and told her to play her first song.

Pain shot up her arm as Libby pressed the keys, and she could not move her hand.

"What is it, Elizabeth? Have you forgotten the notes in that piece? It's very simple."

Tears stung Libby's eyes as she forced herself to play the song. She didn't want Rachael to think she wasn't good enough to keep as a pupil! Someday she—Elizabeth Gail Johnson—would be a concert pianist, and everyone would come to listen to her play. Rachael had said that she was good enough to become a concert pianist because she had the dedication, the determination, and the dream. The past several weeks of lessons with Rachael had improved her playing a lot. Nothing was going to stop the lessons! Especially not a little pain in her right arm!

As she played, the pain increased until she could barely sit still. Several times she fumbled, and Rachael made her repeat the notes.

"Are you sure you practiced enough this week, Elizabeth?" Rachael looked at her with a slight frown, a question in her green eyes. "I know with your work in seventh grade that you don't have the time you had during the summer, but you insisted you could make the time. You wouldn't tell me that you'd practiced just to keep me from being upset, would you?"

Libby shook her head in embarrassment.

"I did practice! I'm just having a little trouble right now. I'll be fine next week."

Just then something crashed in another room, and a baby wailed loudly. Rachael jumped up, saying that she'd better see what her young son had gotten into. "I left him in the nursery with the neighbor girl, but he is getting to be quite a handful."

Libby slumped forward with a sigh as Rachael hurried away. Carefully she rubbed her arm, looking at it with a frown. She felt a hard lump, but she could not see a bruise. It would be all right. It had to be.

She got up and walked around the music room, then stopped in front of the pictures of Rachael in concert. Libby remembered the time she'd come to be interviewed to see if Rachael would take her as a student. Vera and Chuck had brought her and waited in the living room, almost as anxious as she was. Chuck had told her that having a dream was nothing unless you set about fulfilling that dream. And Libby was determined to!

Someday she would sit in front of hundreds of people and play the piano and they would stand and clap until their hands were sore. They would say, "Can this really be the little welfare girl whose father deserted her when she was three and whose mother beat her and deserted her? How can such a nobody become somebody so important, so talented?"

Libby smiled dreamily. She could almost hear the applause for her. The Johnson family would be proud of her and glad that they had prayed her into their home, then adopted her.

She gasped and turned away from the pictures, her eyes wide. They had not adopted her yet. They were waiting for their day in court. What if she did something that would make them change their minds? What if they got mad at her for trying to help April and May Brakie?

Slowly Libby sank back down on the piano bench. She pressed her hands against her thighs and felt the rough denim of her blue jeans. The pain in her arm shot almost to her shoulder, and she moved it until the pain eased. If she held her arm just right in front of her, close to her body, it didn't hurt.

Rachael walked in with a laugh. "Seth was investigating again." She sat down, her dark green skirt falling over her knees. "Ready to try again, Elizabeth? I want you to work on this one." She moved the book so Libby could see the page better. "Your mother will be here soon, and we don't want to keep her waiting."

Libby bit the inside of her lower lip and forced herself to repeat the song. Tears stood in her eyes, and she would not look at Rachael when Rachael told her it was much better and that she should practice it again for next week.

"Your first recital is in November. Keep up the good work, and you will make me very proud of you."

"I will."

"Are you all right? You look pale."

Libby shrugged. "I'm anxious to get my songs just right for you."

"You'll do just fine as long as you practice." Rachael showed her the new songs that she'd have and helped her through them once. "If at any time you get tired of practicing, just remember your dream, Elizabeth. You can't reach the top without working at it."

"I'll work hard." Libby reached for her jacket with her left arm. She could not put it on without Rachael knowing about her injured arm. She carried her music and her jacket to the front door, then turned with a forced smile. "See you next Saturday."

"Tell your mother hello for me."

Libby nodded with a real smile. It felt great to have Rachael call Vera Johnson her mother. Rachael knew that she was a foster girl and that her real mother was Marie Dobbs.

"Better put on your jacket. It's chilly today, Elizabeth."

"It'll be warm in the car, Rachael. Bye." She hurried out the door before Rachael insisted she put on her jacket.

The cool wind cut through her striped top, and she thankfully slid into the warm car at the curb.

"How did it go, honey?" asked Vera with a wide smile. Her blonde hair was pulled back and pinned in a knot at the nape of her neck. She looked young and pretty to Libby, not hard and worldly the way her real mother always looked. Vera smelled like the roses that she grew in the backyard. Mother's perfume had made Libby sick to her stomach.

"Rachael said to practice more. My first recital is in November."

"Does that worry you?" Vera pulled away from the curb and drove down the street, then turned onto the highway toward home.

"It doesn't worry me, Mom. I just wonder if . . ." Her voice trailed away.

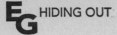

"Wonder what?" Vera looked over at her and lifted her eyebrow.

"Will I be a Johnson by then, do you think?" She waited without breathing.

"I don't know, honey. I hope so. Toby's adoption went through fast, and there's no reason that yours won't too."

Libby sighed in relief and leaned back, holding her arm carefully against her.

"How about going for a hamburger for lunch, Elizabeth?"

Libby was ready to agree when she remembered April and May waiting for her. "I want to get right home, Mom."

"Are you sick? I've never had you turn down a burger, fries, and a chocolate shake before." Vera laughed, but Libby caught the concerned look she threw her.

"I'm all right, Mom. I want to work awhile with Snowball and do some other things." Like feeding the Brakie twins!

Oh, what was she going to do about April and May?

A Big
Decision

LIBBY flicked on the barn light and quickly shut the door, leaving Rex outdoors whining to be let in. "Go away, Rex," she said sharply.

Taking a deep breath, Libby walked down the aisle to the back of the barn, where the bales of hay were stored. Snowball nickered. The smell of the food in the bag she carried almost overpowered the pungent odor of the barn.

"April. May. I brought you something to eat." Libby stopped beside the bales of hay and waited, her heart suddenly racing. Maybe they'd left already. Maybe they'd thought she wouldn't help them. It might be better that way. They could talk to Mrs. Blevins and ask for other foster parents.

Before Libby turned to go, she decided she'd better call again. "April. May." Her voice was sharp and impatient; she wished with all her might that they would be gone. "April! May!"

Two heads popped up from behind the hay. April smiled hesitantly, and May rubbed sleep from her eyes.

"I brought food," said Libby, setting the bag of food on the hay. "I thought you might be gone."

She watched the girls dig into the sloppy joes. Libby waited impatiently while the girls wolfed down the food, then drank the milk she'd poured into two covered plastic glasses. Susan had almost caught her fixing the food, but she'd only been looking for a pencil and had left the kitchen as soon as she'd found one.

Red sauce from the sandwich had dripped down May's chin, and she rubbed it with the back of her hand. "We were hungry," she said finally. "We were very hungry."

"Will you help us, Libby?" April's eyes were sharp and pleading as she turned to Libby.

Libby bent to pick up a gray barn cat that rubbed around her legs. Absently she stroked his dusty fur and he purred loudly.

"Are you going to help us, Libby?" asked May earnestly, her face showing her worry.

Libby licked her dry lips and hugged the cat tighter. "I thought about it a lot, girls. Honest. But I can't do it. I can't take the chance of messing up my life. I want the Johnsons to adopt me. They love me! And I love them."

"Oh, please, Libby, won't you help us?" cried May as tears filled her eyes, then rushed down her cheeks, leaving stains on her dirty face.

"Can't you understand?" Libby's voice rose. She forced it back down in case someone was in the yard and close enough to hear her. "I can't do anything! Do you really think the Johnsons would take you in just because I asked them to? Do you think the family you were staying with will give you up? Go back to them and tell them you're sorry for running away and you won't do it again."

The cat squirmed in Libby's arms and she released him. He jumped to the floor and streaked out of sight into another stall. "I'm sorry, April. I'm sorry, May. I really am." She wanted to run away when she saw the sad looks in their eyes.

April grabbed Libby's arm, and she cried

out in pain until finally April released her. "Libby! Libby, it's Morris Stern! Do you really mean you'll send us back to him?"

"I would rather die," whispered May fiercely, holding her green jacket tightly around her thin body. "Morris Stern, Libby!"

The name bounced around inside Libby's head until she wanted to scream. She backed away, her face white, her eyes wide. "I don't know him."

May stepped toward her, hay clinging to her jeans and jacket. "You know him, Libby. You wish you didn't, but you do."

Libby numbly shook her head. "No," she whispered hoarsely. "No!"

"Miss Miller got you away from him, Libby. You told us all about it. Miss Miller couldn't prove he'd done anything to you, but you know what he tried." May's eyes blazed as she clamped her hands on Libby's shoulders. "Morris Stern! He touched me, Libby. He touched me just the way he did to you, only Mrs. Blevins won't believe me and won't let us leave them."

"He tried with me too, Libby," said April sharply, "but I kicked him and bit him and he left me alone."

Libby's legs gave way and she sank to the

floor, her back tight against one of the horses' stalls. She covered her face with her hands as wave after wave of shame broke over her. She would *not* remember Morris Stern! She didn't dare!

She would think of Miss Miller taking her from that home and finding another home for her. She would remember the day Miss Miller had brought her to the Johnson farm. She had not wanted to come, but soon she'd learned that she was wanted here. They had said they'd prayed her into the family. They believed in God. They believed in praying. She had learned to love Jesus. And she knew that Jesus was with her always—helping her, loving her.

Finally Libby lifted her head and looked at the girls. She saw the concern on their faces as she slowly stood up. "Okay. I'll help you. I will hide you until I figure out how I can help you."

Tears of relief spilled down May's cheeks again, and April knuckled her eyes, then smiled gratefully.

"We couldn't bring any clothes with us," said April, looking at her dirty jeans. "We haven't had a bath since we left two days ago."

"I'll sneak you into the house and hide you in my room. You can take showers when I do." Doubt about getting the girls into the house tried to push its way into her thoughts, but Libby refused to allow it to stay. She would find a way.

"Elizabeth!"

Libby jumped, ready to tell the girls to hide before Ben found her in the barn, but they were already diving out of sight.

"What are you doing, Elizabeth?" Ben stood in the open barn door. The sun shone on his red hair, making it brighter. His blue jacket made his blue eyes look even bluer. "I've been looking all over for you."

She hurried toward Ben, wondering anxiously if she should tell him about the twins. If he knew, would he help? She could not take the chance. He might think it was wrong to hide the girls.

"What do you want?" she asked as she turned off the light and closed the door. She stood beside him in the barnyard. He was a year older than Libby and a little taller than she was, but just as thin. Dad called them his two string beans.

"I wanted you as my partner in Ping-Pong. Susan and Kevin want to see if they can beat us." He laughed and she liked the sound of it. "They sure don't like to lose."

"Neither do we." She walked along beside him and tried to act as cheerful as he expected her to be. "We beat them a lot, but they beat us a few times too."

On the back porch she started to pull off her jacket, then stopped as pain shot through her arm. "I forgot, Ben. I have something important to do. I can't play with you right now."

He frowned. "What's wrong?"

"I just can't play with you. Maybe tomorrow afternoon."

Libby wanted to give in when he begged her, but she couldn't because of her arm. Finally Ben walked away in a huff, and she was afraid he'd be mad for a long time.

Slowly Libby pulled off her jacket and hung it up with her left hand. How much longer would her arm hurt like this?

Piano music drifted from the family room. Libby stood quietly, listening to Vera play. Libby leaned against Chuck's red-plaid farm coat with a sigh. If her arm stayed the way it was, she'd never learn to play as well as Vera.

"It will be just fine," she told herself fiercely. "I know it will!"

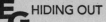

She looked out the porch window toward the horse barn. Right now she had more important things to think about. She had to find a way to smuggle two girls into the house and up to her bedroom. Oh, what had she gotten herself into this time?

Trouble

LIBBY held the telephone receiver tightly against her ear. "Answer your phone, Adam," she whispered urgently. She didn't want Grandma Feuder or Adam's parents to answer.

When Adam answered, Libby sank in relief onto the kitchen chair next to the phone. "Adam, I need your help."

"Sure. What?"

"I need a few minutes to myself. Could you invite the others to your place for a while this afternoon? Is Grandma there? Could you ask Vera to come too?"

From the silence on the other end of the line Libby knew Adam was trying to think ahead of her to figure out why she was going to need time alone.

"What are you up to this time, Elizabeth?" He sounded very suspicious.

Libby forced a laugh. "Will you do it for me, Adam? Please?"

"First tell me what you're up to."

"I can't." She wanted to tell somebody, but she couldn't. Adam would probably keep her secret, but she couldn't take a chance. "Please, Adam."

He sighed and she knew he would do it. He had been her friend ever since she'd taken care of Teddy, Grandma Feuder's special brown teddy bear, for her. Teddy was sitting on her bed beside her toy dog Pinky right now. She would keep him forever!

A half hour later Vera found Libby in the family room. "Are you sure you want to stay here while we go to Feuders', Elizabeth? We won't be long. You can practice when we get back."

"I want to stay home, Mom." She stood with her back to the fireplace. She smiled and Vera kissed her flushed cheek, telling her she'd see her later and to call if she needed them home for any reason.

When the door closed behind them, Libby sighed in relief. Grandma Feuder lived down the road with her great-grandson Adam. She wasn't really related to Libby or the Johnsons, but everyone called her Grandma.

Finally Libby rushed to the barn with Rex at her heels. She called to the twins and hurried them from the barn and into the house. Had anyone seen them?

"Oh, it's warm in here!" cried April with a laugh. "I forgot what it felt like to be warm." She sneezed, then sneezed again.

"I brought the bag of garbage in from our lunch," said May, holding up the bag.

"Come into the kitchen and have something to eat before you go upstairs. I won't be able to get food to you after supper." Libby's legs trembled as she led the way to the kitchen. How could she get away with this? With all the people who lived in this house, someone would see the twins. If it were summer she could have left them in one of the barns.

"What a house!" cried April, looking around the kitchen with wide brown eyes. "I see why you like living here. Me and May would like this place."

"Do you have a bedroom of your own, Libby?" asked May as she poured herself a glass of milk.

Libby described her comfortable bedroom

and told them about the big pink dog that Susan had given her because she was so excited about having a sister.

"What's Susan like?" asked April, sitting at the kitchen table. She bit into her peanut butter and jelly sandwich as Libby sat down across from her.

Libby smiled and shrugged. "Susan is 12, the same as we are."

"We're 13 now," said May, sitting down with a large sandwich in her hands.

"I'll be 13 on February 14," said Libby, remembering all the times she was teased for being a Valentine sweetheart. "Susan is a nice sister to have. She's short and cute and has long red-gold hair. She gets mad at me sometimes."

Libby hurried the girls with their food, then took them upstairs to her room. "If you hurry, you can both take a shower while I find clean clothes for you." Her hands shook as she rummaged through her drawer for clean clothes. What if the family came back sooner than she thought they would? "Please, girls, hurry with your showers."

April sneezed and pressed her hand against her head. "Do you have any aspirin, Libby?"

"Look in the medicine cabinet, April. Just hurry!"

Libby pushed the clean clothes into the girls' arms and watched them walk down the carpeted hallway. Quickly she picked up their jackets and shoes and pushed them behind a box in her closet.

"What am I doing?" she said in agony. "Oh, dear! What am I doing?"

Slowly she walked to her desk and rubbed her finger across the shiny top of the puzzle box that her real dad had sent her. He was dead now, but she had been able to forgive him for deserting her when she was three. Jesus had helped her forgive and love him.

Libby stiffened. Had the door downstairs opened and closed? Was someone home? She waited tensely, listening with her head cocked, her left arm supporting her sore right arm.

Libby jumped nervously when the grandfather clock in the downstairs hall bonged four times. She heard a car drive past on the road in front of the house; then all was quiet except for the sound of running water in the bathroom. When the water stopped, Libby heard only her own breathing.

Libby sank onto the large, round hassock and rocked back and forth. What if Vera and Chuck learned about April and May and got so angry with her that they wouldn't want to adopt her anymore? It wasn't too late for them to change their minds. They could call Ms. Kremeen to come and get her and find another foster home for her. Ms. Kremeen would love to get her away from this Christian home. The social worker had often said that she didn't like all the religious teaching Libby was getting from the Johnsons.

Just then April and May walked into Libby's room, carrying their dirty clothes. Both girls had towels wrapped around their heads. Libby's clothes fit them as well as their own. April had on Libby's yellow sweatshirt and a pair of blue jeans, and May was dressed in a red sweatshirt and blue jeans. Their feet were bare.

"I'm clean!" cried May, dropping her clothes, holding up her hands, and twirling around. "I'm clean again!"

"Not so loud," said Libby with a frown. "What if someone heard you?"

"Is someone here besides us?" asked April, looking around in alarm.

"No," said Libby sharply. "But you will have to get used to the idea of being quiet. I could get in bad trouble if anyone finds you here."

"We're already in bad trouble," said April.

Libby flushed. "I know you are. You stay in my room while I clean up the bathroom and the kitchen. Lock the door. I'll take the key and let myself in when I come up later. But hide when you hear the key in the door in case someone is with me."

Just as Libby reached the door, May said, "Libby."

Libby turned around.

"Libby, thanks. You saved our lives."

"Yea, you did, Libby," added April. "Thanks."

Libby nodded, then rushed from the room before she burst into tears. Why couldn't April and May find a good home? Why didn't Mrs. Blevins hunt until she found them a family like the Johnsons? Why couldn't all the foster kids find Christian homes with people who really loved them and helped them? Oh, she had a lot to be thankful for!

And how was she repaying her new family? She was bringing them trouble! She would have to ask April and May to leave tomorrow while they were in church. Mrs. Blevins would believe them if they insisted that they wanted another foster family.

Libby worked fast in the bathroom, then

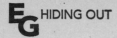

rushed down to the kitchen. She remembered how Mrs. Blevins had tried to take baby Amy away from Lisa Parr because Mrs. Blevins didn't believe that Lisa could take care of her baby.

Libby continued to think as she leaned against the sink and washed the dirty glasses. She was afraid that Mrs. Blevins wouldn't help April and May. Mrs. Blevins might force them to live with Morris and Evelyn Stern no matter what May told her.

Libby bit her lip nervously. She couldn't send the twins back to that family. She would face whatever trouble came! The Johnsons would not let her down.

More Pain

"I'D still like to know who used my shampoo," muttered Susan to Libby as they carried dirty dinner dishes into the kitchen.

"You know Mom said to drop the subject, Susan."

Libby could barely concentrate on what Susan was saying. Her arm was hurting again from carrying the pile of dessert plates. She wanted to get Susan's mind off the missing shampoo, but her brain wouldn't work fast enough.

"Who would use my shampoo? Who would use Kevin's hairbrush? I think something funny is going on around here." Susan piled the dishes in the dishwasher with a thoughtful frown. "I think we should investigate this. What do you think, Libby?"

Libby pressed her sore arm against herself. "What's to investigate? We have better things to do." What if Susan started snooping around? What if she found the twins upstairs? Had Vera missed the food they'd eaten while the family was at church this morning?

"Oh, Libby! You're no fun at all today! Go get the rest of the dishes off table. At least Mom won't let you out of that."

Libby hurried back to the dining room. She knew Susan was upset because Vera had said that Libby could stay in bed a little longer if she really didn't feel well and Susan would do her chores. And she hadn't felt well. The twins had kept her whispering long past bedtime, and during the night she'd had a nightmare that she wouldn't let herself remember. Her arm had been very painful when she'd dressed in her light blue jumper for church. April had had to help her with the zipper.

Impatiently Libby pushed aside her thoughts and carried the dishes to the kitchen, making several trips so her arm wouldn't ache too much. She reached for the last item on the table, Vera's favorite white ironstone platter that had held the roast.

"How's my girl?"

Libby jumped, then looked over her shoulder at Chuck. His red hair was mussed from running his fingers through it. He'd changed from his church clothes into a dark blue shirt and faded jeans. "I thought you were taking a nap, Dad."

"I couldn't yet. I wanted to talk to you."

Her heart froze and then zoomed to her feet. Had he seen the twins in her bedroom? "Have I done something wrong?" she asked in alarm.

Chuck laughed and turned her to him, resting his hands on her shoulders. "Why would you think that? I wanted to make sure you were feeling better, that's all."

"Oh."

"And are you?"

She shrugged. "I guess so." Her right arm was still very painful, but she couldn't tell Chuck about it or he'd insist that she rest it and not play the piano. Maybe she'd have to stop lessons altogether.

He smiled, and laugh lines spread from the corners of his eyes to his hairline. "You don't seem sure." The smile faded and he looked deep into her eyes. "Elizabeth, never be afraid to share your feelings with your mom and me. We want to help you with any problem you might have—large or small. We care about you, about what hurts you, about what makes you happy. I can see that something is bothering you a great deal. Would you like to talk about it?"

Oh, she wanted to! She opened her mouth, then closed it and slowly shook her head. She had to find a way to help the twins without Chuck's help. He would not approve of helping runaways, of hiding them from Mrs. Blevins and the Sterns.

"What is it, Elizabeth?" His voice was low and tender.

Libby wanted to rest her head on his broad shoulder and tell him everything. But instead, she said stiffly, "I have to take this platter to the kitchen."

He kissed her cheek and smiled. "Remember, I'm ready to help with your problem anytime you're ready."

Tears stung her eyes as she bent her head and picked up the heavy platter. She knew he was watching her, giving her another chance to talk to him, but she turned toward the kitchen. The platter was heavy and the pain in her arm increased.

"What took you so long?" asked Susan sharply as she reached for the platter. She bumped Libby's sore arm, and the platter fell into the sink, shattering loudly.

"Look what you made me do!" cried Libby, shoving Susan hard enough to send her staggering across the room to land against the kitchen table.

"I didn't do anything!" screamed Susan, her hands on her hips, her blue eyes blazing. "You're so touchy today that I can't even look at you without making you mad."

"I am not!"

"What trouble are you in this time, Libby?"

"Shut up!"

"Did you use my shampoo and Kevin's hairbrush?" Susan stepped closer and glared into Libby's pale face. "Did you?"

"What if I did? What will you do to me? Who cares about your stupid strawberry shampoo and Kevin's brush? Who cares about anything?"

"You sure don't, do you? You're acting just like you did when you first moved here. You think you're such hot stuff just because you're a welfare kid. You want everyone to feel sorry for you and baby you."

Libby slapped Susan's cheek, then cried out with pain just as Susan did.

"Girls! Girls, what's going on in here?"

Vera stood in the doorway with a frown on her face and her hands at her waist. "I want this fighting stopped right now. Settle it and apologize to each other. I mean it!"

"*She* started it!" cried Susan, pointing at Libby. "She broke your good platter."

"What?" Vera rushed to the sink where Susan pointed, and Libby wanted to run and hide. "Oh, Libby! That was my grandmother's platter. Oh, dear."

"Susan bumped my arm," snapped Libby, lifting her chin high. "It was her fault that it fell into the sink. Susan's just trying to make trouble for me because she's mad at me."

Slowly Vera lifted the broken pieces from the sink. She turned to Libby and Susan. "Girls, broken platters can be replaced. Broken relationships are much more important. Don't let anger keep you from being kind to each other and loving each other. This platter was important to me, but you both are much more important. Settle your argument and apologize."

Libby hung her head, fighting against the tears. "Mom, I'm sorry about your platter."

"I am too," said Susan, barely above a whisper.

"I know you are. I'm going to put the platter in the garbage while you girls settle the problem between you."

Libby peeked at Susan to find her looking sheepishly at her. "Susan, I'm sorry. I shouldn't have pushed you or yelled at you."

"I'm sorry, Libby. I did bump your arm. I didn't think I bumped it that much."

"You didn't. It . . . it hurts a little. I bumped it yesterday." Libby wanted to take back her words but it was too late. Maybe Susan wouldn't ask about it.

"You didn't really use my shampoo, did you?" Susan asked.

"No."

"Then who did?"

"Can't we just drop it, Susan? I'm sick of talking about your shampoo. I have to shake out the tablecloth and slide the chairs under the table." She turned away before Susan could read the guilt that she knew was in her eyes.

Just as Libby finished, Toby ran in to tell her that Adam was waiting outside to talk to her. "He said he couldn't come in because Grandma Feuder wants him right back home," said Toby breathlessly. "Do you and Adam have a secret?"

Libby stared in surprise at Toby. His freckles seemed to stand out more in his excitement. "Why do you ask that?"

"He said I couldn't hang around and listen to him talk to you." Toby grinned and Libby wrinkled her nose at him. She envied Toby because he'd already been adopted by the Johnsons. At first he'd been afraid of her because she looked a lot like his real sister, who had been mean to him. Now they were good friends even though she was 12 and he was only nine.

"Go find Kevin and play with him," said Libby. "I'll go talk to Adam." She had a feeling that Adam wanted to find out why she'd needed the family out of the house yesterday.

Adam was standing beside his bike in the backyard. He smiled at Libby when she came out. The wind ruffled his brown hair. His eyes looked dark with excitement. She would have been very glad to see him if he had wanted something else.

"I can only stay a few minutes, Elizabeth. Tell me about yesterday. I tried to ask you between Sunday school and church, but you wouldn't let me."

"I sure didn't want you asking me in front of anyone!" She looked across the yard as

Goosy Poosy swayed back and forth in a lazy walk across the yard.

"Then it was a surprise!" He caught her hand and she cried out, making him drop it immediately. "What's wrong?"

"You hurt me."

He frowned. "How?"

"Oh, never mind. Just go home and mind your own business."

"Elizabeth, what's wrong with you? I thought we were friends. You said we were."

"We are, Adam. But right now I can't tell you anything about anything. Can't you understand?" She pressed her sore arm against herself and tried to think of something to say to make Adam feel better. "When I can tell you, I will."

He sighed and stuffed his hands into his jacket pockets. "I could tell Ben that you asked me to get all of you out of the house."

Her eyes widened in fear. "No!"

"Hey. I'm sorry, Elizabeth. Don't look like that. I was teasing. I wouldn't do that to you."

Her shoulders sagged in relief as she looked at Adam.

"I'd better get back home. Grandma's waiting." He lifted his hand and smiled, then turned his bike to go down the long driveway to the road. He looked over his shoulder, and Libby could see him looking up at the upstairs windows. She froze at the look on his face.

"I just saw a girl looking out your window. It wasn't Susan. Who was it, Elizabeth?"

She managed a shaky laugh. "You must be seeing things, Adam. Who would be in my room? Maybe it *was* Susan."

"I know what I saw." He walked his bike toward her. "Are you in some kind of trouble?"

"Of course not!"

"Then why won't you tell me who I saw in your window?"

She stamped her foot. "You didn't see anybody!" The words almost caught in her throat. How could she lie like that? She was a Christian. She should not lie. "Adam, go home. I can't tell you anything."

"Tell me this. Was there a strange girl in your room just now?"

She bit her lip nervously. "Yes," she whispered.

"When you can tell me about it, I'll help you all I can."

"Thank you, Adam. Please, don't tell anyone what you saw. Please!"

"I promise." He smiled and she managed to smile back. "See you on the bus in the morning. You will be going to school, won't you?"

She nodded.

"See you then." He pedaled his bike away. She watched until he reached the road and turned toward his house. She had to trust him. She had no choice.

Slowly she walked back into the house, her head down, her sore arm carefully pressed against herself. How long could she keep April and May hidden? How long before everyone knew her secret?

Snoopy
Susan

LIBBY sat cross-legged in the middle of her bed with Pinky in her arms. She looked at April on the hassock and May on the floor, sitting with her back against the closet door. Both girls were dressed in Libby's nightgowns. "I hope you aren't too hungry," said Libby in a low voice. She didn't want anyone who might be walking past in the hall to hear her.

"I don't feel much like eating," said April. She pressed her hand against her forehead. Her face was flushed red, and her eyes had dark circles around them.

"I'm glad you brought the cookies up." May reached for another one from the bag sitting on the floor.

"We have to think of a plan," said Libby earnestly. "Soon Mom's going to start noticing missing food. And she'll wonder how I could get so many clothes dirty in one day."

April sneezed and said she was cold. Libby tossed her a bathrobe and she slipped it on. May ate another cookie and said she'd had enough.

"I heard that Miss Miller married Luke Johnson," said April. "If she was still at Social Services she'd help us."

Libby nodded. "I didn't like her at first, but I was wrong about her. I call her Aunt Gwen now."

May giggled. "Aunt Gwen! And you once spit in her face and called her all kinds of dirty names."

Ashamed, Libby looked down at her multi-colored bedspread. "I'm different now, girls." She looked up at them and watched the questioning looks pass between them. "I'm a Christian now. I accepted Jesus as my personal Savior. I'm learning how to love others with Jesus' love."

The ticking of the clock on the desk seemed loud in the quiet room. Finally April said, "I knew you were different. May and I once stayed at a home where the folks were

Christians. We thought about becoming Christians, but before we could, we had to move. They couldn't afford to keep us."

"Sometimes I read my Bible that the Gideons gave me in the fifth grade." May twisted her long fingers together. "I can't always understand what I'm reading but I read anyway."

"Chuck reads the Bible to the whole family every evening; then we pray and sing and worship together. At first I didn't like it. I thought it was kind of crazy, but I like it now." Libby rubbed her hand on Pinky's soft fur. "I've had my prayers answered. I didn't think God would listen to me at first since I'm nothing but a foster kid, but Dad said that God loves me just the way I am. He said I am important to God, that I am his creation." She laughed self-consciously. "Me! I'm important to God! It doesn't matter to him that I'm tall and skinny and ugly."

Just then the doorknob turned, and Libby's voice died in her throat. Wildly she motioned for April and May to hide under the bed.

"Libby, open the door."

It was Susan. Libby wanted to scream at her to go to her own room and leave her alone. "What do you want, Susan?"

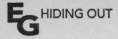

"I heard you talking to someone."

"Go to bed, Susan." Libby stood beside the closed door, her heart racing.

"I'm going to tell Dad if you don't let me in right now." Susan rattled the knob impatiently.

Quickly Libby looked around to see if the twins were out of sight; then she unlocked the door and opened it. "Do you always have to snoop around to see what I'm doing, Susan?"

Susan sailed past Libby and looked around the room. "I heard you talking to someone, Libby. Who's in here? Is that why you've been acting so terrible since yesterday afternoon?"

"What do you mean?" Libby wanted to shove Susan out the door and lock it behind her.

"I know that wasn't a tape playing, Libby. I know you were talking to someone." Susan opened the closet door and peered inside.

Libby grabbed her arm. "What are you doing? Get out of here. I'll tell Dad if you don't!"

Susan's blue eyes flashed angrily. "And I'll tell him that you were talking to someone in here. I'll tell him you have a secret that he needs to know about."

"Oh, Susan! Please, please go to your room. Don't get involved."

Susan clasped her hands in front of herself. "I just want to know your secret, Libby. I won't tell. Honest, I won't. Please tell me. I'm sorry for getting mad at you. I get so tired of having nothing exciting happen to me. Everything exciting happens to you. Please, please, please, tell me what's going on!"

Libby sighed and shook her head. "You don't want to know."

Just then April sneezed. Susan dived under the bed with a gleeful laugh. "Come on out. I know you're under there."

Libby closed and locked her bedroom door, then told April to come out. Susan laughed, looking from Libby to April. When May crawled out, Susan's mouth dropped open in amazement.

"Girls, this is my new sister, Susan. She's all right. She won't tell on you."

"Twins?" whispered Susan in awe.

"I'm April and this is May."

Susan giggled. "April and May? Where's June and July?"

May rolled her eyes. "We're always asked that. Our mother had April just before midnight on April 30 and me a few minutes after midnight on May 1. So she named us April and May."

"How did you get here?" asked Susan, pulling her bathrobe tightly around herself.

"Mostly we walked. Sometimes we rode. Not many people will pick up hitchhikers." April sank down on the edge of the bed and sneezed again. "Oh, my head!"

"Are you sick?" asked Susan in concern.

"Just a cold," said April. She pulled a hanky out of her pocket and blew her nose. "I'll be all right."

Susan sat in the chair by the desk. "How did you girls know to come here?"

Libby looked nervously at the door while the twins told Susan their story. What if someone stopped outside her door just as Susan had done and heard them? "Girls, we have to get to bed. Dad will come up in a little while."

"Where will you sleep?" asked Susan with a frown.

"Under Libby's bed," said May.

"Libby, why didn't you put them in the guest room? Nobody would think of looking in there." Susan walked to the door. "Come on. We'll take them there now."

Libby caught Susan's arm. "Wait. How do you know no one will look in there?"

Susan shrugged. "Who would? They can lock the door and if someone tries to open it, they could hide under the bed. Come on." She unlocked and opened the door and peeked out.

Libby's heart beat like a drum. What if one of the boys walked out into the hallway just then? Her mouth felt dry as she followed Susan and the twins to the guest room. She let her breath out in a loud sigh once they were in the room.

"I'll like sleeping in a bed tonight," said April, already pulling back the covers. "Now I can get warm and get rid of this cold."

"I hope you girls can stay out of sight tomorrow while we're in school," said Libby anxiously as both girls climbed into bed. "I don't know what Mom would do if she found you in the house."

"Mom is going to be gone most of the day tomorrow at a church meeting," said Susan, smiling. "You girls will have the house to yourselves. You can watch TV and eat when you're hungry and everything."

May smiled. "Thanks. We'll make sure we clean up after ourselves."

"How long are you staying?" asked Susan.

"Not long," cut in Libby before April

could say what she'd started to say. "We're going to find a way to help them; then they'll leave."

May wrinkled her nose. "Or we'll ask the Johnson family to take us in. If they can stand Libby, they can stand us."

"Thanks," said Libby, but she laughed, knowing that May was teasing. "We'll see you right after school tomorrow. Stay out of the way of the boys. They won't keep a secret."

"It was nice to meet you, April and May," said Susan. "Sleep well." She smiled, and Libby could tell she was loving every minute of this adventure.

Libby turned off the light and twisted the knob so that when she closed the door it was locked. She sighed in relief. The twins were taken care of for now.

"Why aren't you girls in bed?"

Libby almost jumped out of her skin at Ben's question. Had he seen them come out of the guest room? Did he suspect something? "We're going to bed right now, Ben. Good night."

"Good night, Benjamin," said Susan with a giggle that made Libby want to shake her. Why couldn't she act normal? What if Ben questioned her and got the story out of her?

Ben shook his head. "Girls. Always giggling," he said as he walked to his room.

Libby breathed a sigh of relief. "Stop that, Susan," she whispered. "Go to bed and forget this whole thing."

"I'm going to bed, but I won't forget any of it. I can't wait to get home from school tomorrow afternoon to talk to them again."

Libby clenched her fists and started to snap at Susan. Then she stopped herself, remembering what Mom had said yesterday about being kind and loving. "Good night, Susan. Don't talk in your sleep."

"You either. You probably have a lot more to say than I would." Susan smiled, walked into her room, and closed the door.

Slowly Libby walked to her room and climbed into bed, pulling the covers up under her chin. Susan was right. She did have a lot of things that she could say in her sleep, but she wouldn't.

She turned on her side, then back on her back to keep from hurting her arm. If it wasn't better by tomorrow, she'd have a hard time holding a pencil and writing in school.

Just as she drifted off to sleep her mind clicked to Morris Stern, and she could not lock it back in place. She moaned and covered her eyes, but the picture was behind her eyelids and it refused to leave.

Suddenly she was with Morris Stern. He was holding her in his lap and hugging her and kissing her and she was liking it. She wanted a daddy to love her. But all at once it wasn't like a daddy's hold. She tried to break free, but he was too strong for her. She could smell his stale tobacco breath and feel the stubble of his whiskers.

Then a door had slammed, and she knew Evelyn Stern was home. He pushed her away and told her to get into bed immediately. He said if she ever told, she'd be sorry. But she'd told Miss Miller anyway, and Miss Miller had believed that something was very wrong in that house and had taken her from that home.

Libby jerked and clutched Pinky tightly. She was awake and safe. She was not with Morris Stern. Chuck Johnson was her dad. He didn't do what Morris Stern had done. Chuck loved her and treated her like a daughter.

Tears filled her eyes and streamed down her cheeks, and the bed shook with her sobs. She would not think about Morris Stern again! She would not! She would push that memory back in place and lock it in her head so it would stay hidden forever!

Ms. Kremeen

"I FINALLY figured it out, Elizabeth." Adam leaned close to Libby so that no one else on the school bus could hear him. "Somebody is blackmailing you. You have to keep quiet about that girl or you'll be killed in your sleep."

"Adam!" Libby didn't know whether to laugh or scold.

"Am I right?"

"No!" She frowned and stared out the window at the passing countryside as they headed home. She had tried to avoid Adam all day at school, but he'd caught her on the bus, and she didn't know how to stop him from asking questions.

He nudged her. "Are you in danger?"

She turned to him in exasperation. "Of course not! Will you just drop it? I said I'd tell you when I could. I can't yet."

He shifted his English and math books. "You know you're driving me crazy. Just try to tell me when you *can* tell me what's going on."

She leaned her head back wearily. "Tomorrow. Maybe the next day. At least by Saturday."

"I can't wait," Adam groaned, sliding lower in his seat. "You're turning me into an old man."

She knew what he meant. She felt like an old woman—at least 40. This morning Mom had asked if she was sure she felt well enough to go to school, but if she'd stayed home, Vera would've stayed with her. That would have been too nerve-racking.

Libby smoothed her navy pants over her legs, then carefully laid her arm in her lap. She had been able to write in school as long as she hadn't gripped her pencil too tightly. At home she planned on practicing the piano no matter how much it hurt her arm. She had to keep her evening as normal as possible. And she'd have to keep Susan from popping wide open and telling everything. Several times in school Susan had whispered something about the twins and Libby had had to hush her. Susan had a very hard time keeping a secret.

Just then Susan nudged Libby from behind. "We're almost home," she hissed. "I can't wait."

Libby closed her eyes tightly. Why couldn't Susan keep quiet? Would Adam realize that Susan knew something?

"Libby. Libby, what's wrong?" asked Susan. "Aren't you excited? How can you just sit there? I feel like jumping up and down."

Libby swung around to face Susan with an angry frown. "What's so special about tonight? We're going to do our chores and homework same as usual."

Susan seemed to shrink inside herself, and she mumbled something Libby couldn't catch.

"Why are you mad at her?" asked Adam sharply.

"Mind your own business," snapped Libby; then softly she added, "Adam, don't talk to me right now. I have too much on my mind."

"I can see that." He opened his English book and started reading. When the bus stopped at the Johnsons' driveway, he looked up. "If you need any help, call me."

Libby felt about two feet high. "Thanks," she whispered. She stepped around his legs and followed the others out of the bus.

The warm sun shone down on her, and she pulled off her jacket carefully, making sure she didn't twist or bump her right arm. The others ran on ahead, but Susan stayed with her, walking quietly beside her.

A small yellow car stood in the driveway near the front door. Libby stopped, her heart pounding like a kettledrum. The car belonged to Ms. Kremeen!

Libby turned and glared at Susan. "You told! You told, and she's come to take me away and take the twins back to the Sterns'. Mrs. Blevins is probably with Ms. Kremeen!"

"Libby!" Susan grabbed her arm, and she winced in pain. "Libby, I didn't tell anyone. Ms. Kremeen is probably here for her usual visit to see about you."

"Why today?"

"I don't know. Let's find out."

Libby's mouth was dry. "Oh, what if Mom found the twins and called Ms. Kremeen? I thought you said Mom would be gone for the day."

"But she had to come home to be here when we got home. Calm down, Libby.

You're getting upset for nothing." Susan's red-gold hair bounced around her slender shoulders and hung down her back over her yellow jacket.

Libby nodded. "Maybe you're right. I'll talk to Ms. Kremeen and find out what she wants. I don't dare walk in there expecting her to know about the twins, because if she doesn't know, she'd see I have a secret."

"I'll stay with you, Libby. If she does know about the twins, I'll try to get them out of the house and away so they won't have to go back to that terrible family."

Libby managed a smile. "Thanks, Susan."

Susan wrinkled her small nose. "I want to help."

Libby's legs felt almost too weak to carry her into the house. Upon entering, she smelled fresh-baked cookies and wondered how long Vera had been home.

"Elizabeth." Vera stood in the study door and motioned for Libby to join her.

Slowly Libby walked to the study with Susan close behind her. A shiver ran down her back. The grandfather clock bonged four o'clock.

"Ms. Kremeen wants to talk to you, Elizabeth." Vera slipped her arm around Libby's shoulders. "Susan, run to the kitchen and have milk and cookies with your brothers."

Libby saw Susan hesitate, then turn away toward the kitchen.

Inside the study Ms. Kremeen sat on the chair behind Chuck's large oak desk. She nodded to Libby and asked her to sit down.

Thankfully Libby did. She knew her legs wouldn't support her another minute. Vera sat beside her on the couch and crossed her legs, her khaki skirt falling over her knees. Libby could see Vera's hands clasped tightly together in her lap. What had they been talking about?

"How was school, Libby?" asked Ms. Kremeen in a brisk, businesslike voice. Her gray eyes looked cold and hard. Her long auburn hair waved attractively around her pretty face.

"It was all right," said Libby, dropping her eyes to the tips of her stockinged feet.

"I heard that you're having trouble in reading."

Libby's head shot up. "I am not!"

"Libby," warned Vera, patting Libby's leg gently. "Don't get upset."

"Who said I was having trouble in reading?" Libby asked, forcing her voice to sound normal, not angry or rebellious. Ms. Kremeen was trying to find a way to get her away from the Johnsons.

"I called the school and talked to Mrs. Kayle." Ms. Kremeen folded her hands on the desk and leaned forward. "She said you haven't been doing the work she assigns you."

Libby opened her mouth to speak, but Vera interrupted. "Elizabeth is taking special tutoring to help her reading, Ms. Kremeen. She is doing the best she can. I work with her at home also. I don't think you have to worry about her reading."

Ms. Kremeen cleared her throat. Libby could see the anger boiling inside her. Did Vera realize how angry she was? Libby peeked at Vera, then away. If she knew, she didn't care. Libby tried to relax, but couldn't.

"Mrs. Johnson, I would like to talk to Libby alone."

"No, Ms. Kremeen. I'm staying here with her. Whatever you have to say to her, I want to hear."

Libby hid a little smile. She knew it had been hard for Vera to say that. Dad would have said it without any problem, but Mom wasn't as brave as Dad was.

"I must insist, Mrs. Johnson." Ms.

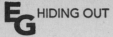

Kremeen stood up, her fists knotted tightly at her sides, her head high. She was dressed in a gray, pin-striped pants suit with a white tailored blouse. Libby thought she was going to explode.

Vera leaned back with a smile. "Insist away, Ms. Kremeen. I am staying. I know that you don't approve of Libby's living with us because of our belief in God. I know that you want to get her away from us before the judge can rule in favor of our adopting her, but nothing you can say will stop it from happening. Elizabeth is ours."

Libby watched the struggle Ms. Kremeen was having with herself. What would happen if she ever lost her poise and control?

Finally Ms. Kremeen sat down again. "Libby, I want to know again if you want to stay here."

"I do."

"I have a family in the city who would very much like to have you with them."

"I'm staying here." Libby said steadily, but she was glad when Vera's hand closed over hers. It helped her stay calm.

"This family has only one daughter," continued Ms. Kremeen in an even voice. "They could give you more time and advantages than the Johnsons can with four children—five counting you."

Libby bit back a giggle as she thought of April and May hiding upstairs. The family had seven children, but only she and Susan knew it. Oh, she was glad neither Ms. Kremeen nor Vera had discovered them!

"Elizabeth is going to stay with us, Ms. Kremeen. We prayed her into this family, and she is going to stay. I will work harder with her on her reading and on whatever else she needs help with. You don't have to worry about her at all."

Ms. Kremeen opened her briefcase and pulled out a folder. "I will drop this discussion for now, but I am not giving up, Mrs. Johnson. I am only pulling back." She opened the folder and looked at it, then lifted her cold, gray eyes to Libby.

Libby squirmed uncomfortably.

"Mrs. Blevins told me that you once lived with the Mason family when April and May Brakie lived there."

Libby sat very still and forced the panic away. She knew Ms. Kremeen's sharp eyes wouldn't miss a flicker of her eyelash. She nodded. "Yes, I know them," she volunteered.

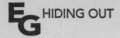

"The twins have run away from their present foster home again. Do you know anything about them?"

"How could she?" asked Vera sharply. "Libby has been here all the time except when she's in school. How can she help you find two runaway girls?"

"We're asking everyone who knew them," said Ms. Kremeen impatiently. "I told Mrs. Blevins I would ask Libby."

Libby did not move. She would not answer unless Ms. Kremeen asked again.

Ms. Kremeen stuffed the folder back into her case and stood up. "I had some business to discuss in private with Libby, but since I'm not allowed to, I'll leave."

Libby was too weak to move.

"Ms. Kremeen, we will not allow you to upset Elizabeth. We know that you wanted her back with her real mother. We know that you will try anything to get her away from us, but you will not succeed. She belongs to us!" Vera kept her gaze steady as she got up. Her blonde hair curled around her head and hung down onto her slender shoulders. Libby could smell her light floral perfume as she walked to the study door with Ms. Kremeen.

Libby sat still in the empty study for a long time, then finally pushed herself off the couch. A smile spread across her face and lit up her hazel eyes. "Thank you, Jesus. Thank you for this wonderful family."

Double
Trouble

LIBBY wanted to grab Toby and shake the freckles off his face. She scowled at him angrily. "I can't do your chores, Toby! I can't!"

"But I want to watch an after-school special!" He looked as if he would burst into tears. "You help Kevin and Ben and Susan when they ask you. Why won't you help me? Do you hate me because the Johnsons already adopted me and not you?"

"Leave me alone, Toby." She walked toward the cow barn, where Ben was milking. She had three calves to feed. If she did her chores, Toby's chores, *and* practiced her piano, she knew her arm would start hurting so much that someone would notice.

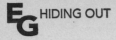

"I bet you won't because of the secret you have in your room," shouted Toby.

Libby whirled around. "What secret?" she said, her voice full of fear. She had been very careful when she'd gone to her room to change after Ms. Kremeen left. She had talked to April and May in whispers. They had said their day had gone just great. May said that once the phone had almost rung off the hook, and she'd had to slap her own hand to keep from answering. April had slept most of the day. She hadn't been able to eat anything, but May said she made up for it.

Toby made a face. "I know you have a secret. I heard Susan talking about it. Kevin knows you have a secret and Ben knows it too, so if you don't do my chores for me, I'll tell Mom."

"You go right ahead and tell! And when Mom doesn't do anything about it, you sit in the corner and pout and suck your thumb!" Libby watched his face turn as red as his hair. He was trying very hard to stop sucking his thumb.

"I hate you, Libby! I hope you never get adopted into this family! I hope you have to go live with the meanest family in the whole world!" He spun around and ran across the yard to Kevin at the chicken house.

Libby trudged to the barn. After the Johnsons learned about April and May, would they send her away? What if she had to live with Morris and Evelyn Stern? She moaned in pain and shook her head. That couldn't happen to her! But she couldn't take a chance on Chuck or Vera learning about the twins. Tonight after everyone was in bed, they would have to leave. No matter what! But where would they go? What if they starved to death or worse, because she wouldn't help them when they needed her?

She walked into the barn, her head down, concentrating on her thoughts. Toby would stay mad at her forever. She couldn't do anything about that. Before long maybe everyone in the whole world would be mad at her.

"Here's the milk, Elizabeth."

Libby looked up with a start as Ben handed the pail of foaming milk to her.

"What's wrong?" asked Ben when she quickly put the milk down on the concrete floor.

"It's heavy." She wanted to rub her arm, but she knew Ben would want to know why.

"I'll help you pour it in the calves' buckets." When he smiled at her, the pain around her heart eased a little. Ben was always very patient with her. He'd taught her to ride a horse when she'd first come to the farm. He'd helped her learn to do outdoor chores when she'd been afraid to try, because she'd never lived in the country before.

She watched as he divided the fresh milk equally among the three buckets. Steam rose from the milk, and Libby wrinkled her nose at the smell. How could the calves drink warm milk without cocoa mixed in it?

Libby carried the buckets one at a time to the large stall where the calves were impatiently waiting. She leaned against the stall's wooden gate and watched as the calves drank the milk, butting their heads against the buckets as they finished. Quickly she pulled the buckets away from them and carried them to the faucet, where she rinsed them clean. A cat rubbed against her leg as she stood the buckets upside down on the shelf made for them.

She turned around to find Ben watching her with a puzzled frown. Her heart skipped a beat, and before she could stop herself, she flushed guiltily.

"Elizabeth, you haven't been yourself since

Saturday. Can't you tell me what's wrong?"
He walked toward her. She pressed her thin
lips tightly together. It was going to be hard to
keep her secret from Ben.

"I see that stubborn look on your face,
Elizabeth. I won't force you to tell me, but
I can't help you if I don't know your prob-
lem."

She turned away, her eyes wide to keep the
tears from falling. Oh, she wanted to tell him!
She wanted him to help her!

"Has Brenda Wilkens been causing more
trouble for you?" Ben asked kindly.

Libby shook her head.

"I didn't think so, since she's a Christian
now. Have you noticed that she's different?"

Libby nodded silently. She had to get away
from Ben before she told everything about
the twins and her arm and the Sterns. "I'm
going to the house, Ben," she said in as
normal a voice as she could.

She went to the barn door, waiting for him
to call her back, hoping that he might force
her to tell him what was bothering her.
Outside the door, she lifted her face to the
evening breeze and breathed in deeply.

Rex barked from where Kevin had tied him
to his doghouse for the night. A horse neighed

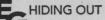

from inside the barn. It sounded like Susan's horse, Apache Girl.

Libby squared her shoulders and walked to the house. She had to face the family at supper, help with the dishes, practice her piano, and then she'd be free to go to her room to talk to April and May. Was Susan with them now? Would she get overexcited and accidently expose the twins?

Libby picked at her supper, causing Vera to ask her if she was feeling sick. Libby said she wasn't very hungry, and she thought to herself that she might never be hungry again if she had to keep worrying about the twins.

By the time she sat down to practice the piano, the pain in her arm was severe. She wanted to go to her room and lie down, but she forced herself to open her piano book. She had to practice! Rachael Avery had said that if she didn't keep up with her practicing, she couldn't continue as a student. Vera had said Rachael was one of the best teachers around, that Rachael would help her turn her dream into a reality.

Pain shot up Libby's right arm as she pressed the keys. "I will not give up!" she muttered to herself.

"Did you say something, honey?" asked

Vera from the doorway. She was drying her hands with a dish towel, and a floral-print apron was tied around her narrow waist.

"I was talking to myself," said Libby. She played the songs in the first book, then opened the second book. How long would her arm feel this way? Would she ever be without pain? Her hands froze on the keys. What if she could never play again? What if she ruined her arm by using it too much while it was hurt? She could not play another minute. Maybe tomorrow her arm wouldn't hurt and she could practice two hours.

Wearily she climbed the carpeted stairs, her hand sliding along the shiny banister. She stopped outside her closed bedroom door. She heard giggling, and she looked quickly around in alarm. What if one of the boys heard the giggling? She turned the knob, her heart almost dropping to her feet. It was unlocked! How could they forget to lock it?

She rushed in, slamming the door shut behind her. Susan and May jumped from the bed, then sank back down.

"You scared me silly," said Susan.

"You forgot to lock the door," snapped Libby.

"Sorry," said May. "We came in here to

talk. April wanted to take a nap. I don't think she feels very good."

"Neither do I!" Libby plopped down on the chair at her desk. "I can't wait until you girls get out of here and away from me."

May picked up Teddy and rubbed his furry arm. "Me and April were making plans today. We could leave the state and live on our own."

"You can't do that!" cried Susan, shaking her head until her ponytail bobbed hard.

May sighed unhappily. "Libby, you've been good to us. I wish we could stay here in this family, but I don't think they can keep us. They don't need two more girls. We've decided to leave tomorrow after you go to school."

Libby sagged back in her chair, then sat up straight. "But how can you live on your own?" She remembered the terrible stories she'd heard of girls on their own. She didn't want anything bad to happen to April and May.

Susan jumped off the bed. "I think we should tell Dad. He'll know what to do. I think we should ask him to find a home for April and May." She turned toward the door but May stopped her.

"You can't! Your dad would turn us in. He

wouldn't believe our story about Morris Stern. I couldn't live if we had to go back there! I would kill myself first." Her brown eyes were wild with fear, and her face was as white as the pillowcase on Libby's pillow.

"She won't tell," said Libby softly. "She's only trying to help." She turned to Susan. "You won't tell, will you?"

Susan stared at May, then slowly shook her head.

"I'm going back to the guest room with April," said May quietly. "We'll leave in the morning for sure."

Libby wanted to scream and cry and make someone change the terrible things in life. She wanted the twins to have a good home to live in with wonderful people to love them and take care of them.

Slowly she opened the door and peeked out. Libby motioned for May to follow her. What would she do if she came face-to-face with one of the boys or with Chuck or Vera? It was too scary to think about. She hurried down the hall, with May and Susan following close behind her.

In relief they closed the guest room door, then moved to the bed where April lay. She looked thinner than the day before. She opened her eyes and tried to smile through her cracked lips.

Libby leaned against the bed, her hands on the fuzzy gold blanket. "How do you feel, April?"

"I'm all right." Her voice came out in a croak. "Did May tell you that we're leaving in the morning? We don't want to get you in trouble. You've got it made here, and we don't want to mess it up for you."

"How can you leave?" asked Susan in alarm. "You're sick. You can't leave while you're sick."

"I'll be all right in the morning." April tried to smile but failed.

Just then the doorknob squeaked slightly as it slowly turned. May dove under the bed but April couldn't move. Libby dashed across the room and reached for the door to slam it shut.

But Toby slipped into the room and looked around with wide eyes. "I knew you had a secret!"

"Get out of here, Toby!" cried Susan angrily. "You get out right now!"

Libby grabbed for his arm but he jerked away and ran to the bed. "I know you. You're April Brakie. My sister Janis stayed in a home with you and your sister once."

May climbed out from under the bed. "Hi, Toby. We heard you were adopted."

"You won't tell, will you, Toby?" asked Libby breathlessly. She nervously rubbed her hands down her jeans.

Toby walked to the door and opened it. "Yes, I'll tell!" He stalked out and slammed the door behind him.

Libby could hear him running down the hall. She stared at Susan and the twins, her thoughts in a panic.

Tattletale Toby

WITH a cry, Libby yanked open the bedroom door and leaped into the hallway just in time to see Toby disappear into Ben's room at the head of the stairs. Susan pushed against her, but Libby told her to stay with the twins and keep them out of sight.

Supper smells still lingered in the air as Libby raced to Ben's room. Oh no! Now she'd never be adopted! She'd probably end up living with the Sterns along with April and May.

Outside the bedroom door Libby could hear Toby's voice, loud with excitement. Libby's chest rose and fell as she tried to catch her breath. Her hand trembled as she reached for the doorknob.

She opened the door and stepped inside, closing the door with a sharp bang. She leaned against it as Toby jumped behind Ben and peeked out from behind him. Kevin stood beside Ben's desk, his eyes wide behind his glasses. He stepped toward Libby, then stopped abruptly.

"Toby, you can't tell," said Libby in agitation. "You can't tell! You don't know what's going on. You'll hurt the girls. You'll hurt me!" She saw the triumph on Toby's face and her heart sank. He was determined to tell because he wanted to hurt her.

"Do you really have two girls hidden in the guest room?" asked Kevin in a hushed voice.

"She does!" cried Toby, nodding hard. "She sure does!"

"Toby!" snapped Ben, gripping his arm. "Let Elizabeth talk."

Toby jerked free, his eyes blazing. "Sure. Libby can talk all she wants. Libby can do anything! I don't care what you say. I'm going to tell Mom and Dad! And I'm telling them right now." He rushed toward the door, but Libby caught him and held him tightly. He squirmed and almost got away.

"Stop it, Toby," she said as she shook him.

"The girls are leaving in the morning. There is no reason to tell. I was helping them, Toby. You can understand that, can't you? Remember how bad Janis treated you? You had to have help to get away from her—your own sister. April and May are in trouble and they need help."

She saw his hesitation, then his firm decision that no matter what she said he was going to tell. She looked across the room at Ben and silently begged him to help her with Toby.

"Don't tell, Toby," said Ben softly. "We'll help Elizabeth with those girls."

Toby stood quietly. Libby smiled in relief as she loosened her grip. He brought his arms up hard and jerked free, shoving her. She stumbled and fell hard against a tall chest, striking her sore arm. She cried out in pain, doubling onto the floor and sobbing in agony.

"Look what you did, Toby," cried Kevin, kneeling beside Libby.

"I don't care!" Toby crossed his arms and glared at them.

"Where do you hurt?" asked Ben, helping her sit up. "Is it your arm?" He touched it and she cried out again, cradling it against her slim body.

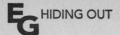

"My arm's broken. I know it. I'll never play the piano again." She rocked back and forth, trying to ease the pain.

"I'm glad!" Toby stood beside her, glaring down at her. "I hope they have to cut it off!"

"Toby!" Kevin grabbed for Toby but he jumped back. "Can't you see she's hurt bad? Stop being so mean."

"She doesn't like me, so why should I like her?" Toby backed against the bed, his face white and his freckles standing out boldly.

Just then the door opened, and Chuck and Vera walked in. Libby wanted the floor to open up and swallow her.

"What is all this yelling!" asked Chuck sternly.

"We heard you clear down in the study," said Vera. "Have you boys hurt Elizabeth?"

"Toby knocked her against the chest and hurt her arm," said Kevin breathlessly. "It might be broken."

Chuck knelt beside Libby and carefully examined her arm. "It isn't broken, just bruised on the muscle right here." He pointed to the swollen place, while Libby felt fresh tears run down her cheeks.

"It looks like you won't be able to use that

arm for a few days, honey," said Vera. "I'll fix a sling so it'll rest completely."

Chuck gripped Toby's shoulder. "We'll go to my study and have a talk, young man."

"No!" cried Libby, struggling to her feet.

"Why not?" asked Chuck with a frown. "What's going on, Elizabeth?"

She moistened her dry lips and knuckled the tears from her eyes. "It was my fault. I was fighting with Toby. He didn't mean to hurt me. Honest, Dad."

"Ben, was it an accident?" asked Chuck, turning to Ben.

Ben nodded.

"Toby was going to tell on Libby," said Kevin. "And she tried to stop him and he pushed her."

"What was he going to tell?" asked Vera, looking from one to the other.

Libby silently pleaded with Toby not to tell on her. She saw by his face that he was hesitating. Ben's clock ticked loudly in the silence.

"Elizabeth. Toby. Both of you come with me to my study." Chuck walked to the door and waited for them. His white pullover fit snugly against his muscled chest and arms.

"I won't let you beat me!" cried Toby, hanging back in fear.

"Toby, have I beat you since you've come to live with us? Has Vera beat you?" Chuck stood with his hands lightly on his narrow hips.

Toby hesitated, then shook his head.

"I will never beat you, Toby. Vera will never beat you. But I do insist on the truth from you. I insist on right behavior, or I'll punish you the same as I punish the other children in the family."

Libby walked toward the door, her head down. Soon everyone in the family would know what she'd done. And she would never be Elizabeth Gail Johnson. She'd be Elizabeth Gail Dobbs forever. She'd be put in a juvenile home, or worse, in the Sterns' home. Her dream of becoming a concert pianist was gone forever! April and May had come to her for help and she'd failed them.

Vera touched her shoulder and Libby jumped. "Are you sick, honey? You look ready to collapse." Vera turned to Chuck. "Why don't we let Libby go to bed. You can talk to her in the morning."

"You'd let Libby off but not me!" cried Toby, his fists doubled at his sides. "You love her more than you do me. Everybody loves Libby more!"

"Let's talk in my study," said Chuck, slipping his arm around Toby, but Toby jerked away and glared at Libby. She knew he was going to tell, and there was no way she could stop him.

With a moan Libby leaned against the door frame.

"I see that we have a real problem here," said Chuck softly. "I think that we need to talk right here, right now. Toby, you start."

Libby bit the inside of her bottom lip to keep from crying out. She could not stop Toby now. Chuck wouldn't let her.

Vera looked around with a frown. "Where's Susan? It isn't like her to miss out on anything." Before anyone could answer, Vera stepped to the door. "Susan. Come here, Susan." She waited, then called louder.

Libby heard a door open and close, and she knew Vera had seen Susan come out of the guest room.

Ben cleared his throat, and Libby looked up at him to find him studying her in concern. She dropped her gaze and stared at Chuck's stockinged feet.

Susan walked guiltily into the room. "Don't

blame Libby, Dad. She was only trying to help them. They had to run away. I helped them too."

Libby stifled a groan as she stared at Susan.

"What are you talking about, Susan?" Chuck asked with a frown.

Susan looked around helplessly. "Didn't Toby tell?"

"Not yet," said Vera. "But he's going to. It looks like this is a family affair, something we'll all want to hear about." She moved to the chair beside Ben's desk and sat down. Libby could tell that she was prepared for anything.

"I think we'd all better sit down," said Chuck; he sat on the edge of Ben's bed. He waited until the others were seated on the carpeted floor.

Libby smiled weakly at Susan beside her. Susan managed a weak smile in return.

"Toby, I think you should start," said Chuck, reaching over to tap Toby's red head.

Libby forced herself to sit still. She wanted to run, but she knew that running wouldn't do any good.

"I don't want to tell," said Toby in a low, tight voice.

"You sure wanted to a while ago," snapped Ben.

"Since you want to talk, Ben, you tell me," said Chuck sternly.

Ben squirmed uncomfortably and shook his head.

"Toby, I want to hear what was so important that you had to hurt your sister," demanded Chuck in a voice that Libby knew meant business.

Toby's eyes seemed huge in his face. "Libby is . . . Libby is hiding . . ." His voice trailed away.

Libby's heart pounded loudly enough that she was sure everyone in the room could hear it. Her stomach cramped tightly. The pain in her arm seemed like nothing now.

"Continue, Toby," commanded Chuck.

"Don't make him, Dad!" cried Susan, twisting her fingers tightly together. "You don't want to know!"

"Oh, dear," said Vera.

"I insist on knowing," said Chuck. "Toby."

Libby wanted to die on the spot.

Toby's eyes filled with tears that slowly slipped down his pale face. "April and May Brakie are here," he mumbled.

"April and May Brakie?" asked Vera with a frown.

"Twins," Susan informed them. "Libby's helping them run away."

"Oh, dear," said Vera again.

"My, my," said Chuck.

Libby sat very still and stared at her knees.

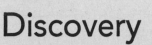

Discovery

LIBBY pulled up her knees and pressed her face against them. She heard Ben's clock and her own breathing. Wasn't anyone going to say anything? She jumped as a hand closed over her shoulder.

"Look at me, Elizabeth."

Slowly she lifted her face and looked up at Chuck. He didn't look as if he hated her. Her hopes rose a little, then crashed back down when she realized that it might be out of his hands. Ms. Kremeen would love to hold this against her and place her in a different home.

"Tell me about April and May Brakie," said Chuck, sitting in front of her on the carpet.

Libby's hand brushed back a stray strand of hair. "They're twins. Twin girls. We lived

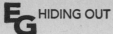

together with the Mason family, and now they live with the Sterns. They're 13." What more could she say? Chuck wouldn't know about men like Morris Stern.

"Why did they run away?"

Libby closed her eyes, then opened them wide. "They want to live somewhere else. They heard I was being adopted, and they came to find me to see if you would adopt them too."

"Why did they run away, Elizabeth?" Chuck caught her left hand and held it firmly.

Libby looked quickly around the room, then back at Chuck. "The man was mean to them."

"Did he beat them?"

She shivered. "No." Oh, she could not think about it, could not let herself remember again! "I told April and May I would help them find a place to live. I thought I could tell Mrs. Blevins to place them with a nice family, a family like this one."

"I think we should talk to the girls," said Vera, standing up. She tugged her gray sweater down over her black pants. A gold chain hung around her neck.

"I want to see them," said Kevin excitedly.

"Did they come Saturday?" asked Ben, a knowing look on his narrow face.

"Yes," said Susan. "Libby found them hiding in the horse barn. She said she thought Marie Dobbs was hiding and waiting to grab her, but she discovered the girls instead."

"I can see you children think this is a great adventure," said Chuck, rubbing his temple, then letting his red hair fall over his wide forehead. He looked at them and shook his head.

"I never have anything exciting happen to me," said Susan defiantly. "It was fun helping Libby hide them."

"I wondered what happened to the food in the refrigerator," said Vera. "And the cookies seemed to disappear right before my eyes."

Chuck got up and took Vera's hand in his. "Let's go talk to Elizabeth's runaways. But I don't think they need all these extra listening ears and watching eyes at our first encounter."

Kevin groaned and Ben begged to go along. Toby asked what the fuss was about, since they were only two girls who looked alike. Susan looked as if she would burst into tears. Chuck told Libby to lead the way.

Libby's legs felt like melting marshmallows as she walked ahead of Chuck and Vera to the guest room. It was already dark inside, so she flicked on the light. May was sitting in a chair by the window. She stared back at her with wide, fearful eyes. She still had on Libby's jeans and a gold sweatshirt. Her hair was in a ponytail. April tried to push herself up in the bed, but then she lay back down.

"Don't make us go back!" cried May in alarm as she stared from Chuck to Vera.

Chuck reached out to pat her arm, but she cringed away from him. He dropped his hand at his side. "We just came to talk to you."

Vera touched April's forehead. "How long have you had this bad cold?"

"A couple of days. I'm all right," said April in a weak voice. "We're leaving in the morning."

When Chuck shot Libby a look, she explained that the girls knew they couldn't live off the Johnson family, that they were going out of state.

Chuck raised his eyebrow, then shook his head. "Who is April and who is May?" he asked.

"I'm May." She pointed to the bed. "She's April. Are you going to call Mrs. Blevins tonight?"

Libby rubbed her arm to ease the pain. What would ease the pain in her heart, in the twins' hearts?

"When did April last eat?" asked Vera, looking from May to Libby in concern.

Libby shrugged and May said she didn't know. "She hasn't been drinking anything," said May. "I told her she should."

"I can't," said April.

"You must have fluids," said Vera. "I'm going to get something for you right now." She hurried from the room, a worried frown on her pretty face.

Libby moved close to Chuck and looked up into his face. "You won't call Mrs. Blevins to get them tonight, will you?"

"Don't! Please, please don't!" begged May.

"Girls, I will call her to let her know that you're safe, but I'll ask her to leave you with me until tomorrow." He smiled. "Relax. We aren't in this alone. God is the head of this house. He guards our lives and our actions. He loves both of you girls, and he wants what is best for you." He rested his hand on April's forehead, and she tried to pull away. "Don't be afraid of me; I won't hurt you."

"He won't," Libby assured April.

"Are you sure?" asked May barely above a whisper, and Libby nodded.

Vera hurried back into the room. "Here's a glass of orange juice. April, you must drink a little of it." She helped April drink, then set the glass on the nightstand beside the bed. "I want you to drink a little as often as you think of it."

"April, the Bible says that God really cares about our problems," said Chuck. "We'll pray for you, if you don't mind."

"All right," she whispered.

Chuck rested his hand on her forehead, and this time she didn't move away. Libby caught May's hand and held it as she bowed her head.

"Heavenly Father, thank you for sending Jesus to us. We ask you, Lord, to take care of April's cold. We know that you want her to be well and strong. Help April to know that you love her and will help her get well. Help May to know you love her too. Thank you that you are answering the girls' needs for a place to live. Thank you that they came to our Elizabeth for help, and that you will show us the best way to help them."

When they finished praying, Libby felt a smile tug at her lips; she hadn't known she could smile in all of this. She saw the tension leave May's face. April drank another swallow of juice and dropped off to sleep.

Chuck smiled at May. "Jesus will take care of April. You don't have to worry about her."

May smiled hesitantly at Chuck, then backed away from him.

"May, when did you last eat?" asked Vera. "Come downstairs with me and I'll fix you something nutritious."

May hung back, her eyes on Chuck. "You won't let Mrs. Blevins take us tonight, will you?"

"No. I'll call Mr. Cinder, and he can contact Mrs. Blevins. He will let you stay here."

"Thanks, Dad," said Libby. She wanted to hug him and tell him she loved him very much, but she followed May and Vera from the bedroom. She stopped in the hallway and waited while Susan introduced May to the boys.

Chuck slipped his arm around Libby's thin shoulders. "I'd like to talk to you in my study while May's eating," he said in a voice too low for the others to hear.

Libby's heart sank. She should have known that she wouldn't get out of it that easily.

"Where's April?" asked Kevin with a chuckle.

"She's asleep," said Vera. "Please don't disturb her. You can meet her in the morning." Her voice was firm and the boys knew they had to obey. They walked to their rooms while Susan followed May and Vera downstairs.

Libby walked with Chuck, and he stopped her outside Toby's room. "We can't settle for the night until we have this problem solved between you and your brother."

Reluctantly Libby entered Toby's room. He was lying on top of his covers sucking his thumb. When he saw them, he jumped up and quickly hid his hand behind his back.

"Toby, I know it's almost your bedtime," said Chuck. "But I don't want you to go to sleep feeling bad toward your sister."

"She's not my sister!"

"Yes she is." Chuck sat on the bed and pulled Toby close to him. "Son, we love you. We prayed you into our family. You are part of us. Elizabeth is part of us too. What has happened to cause this trouble between you two?"

Libby stood quietly beside the dresser. She watched Toby's eyes fill with tears.

"Libby doesn't love me," he whispered.

"I do too!" cried Libby. "Why do you say I don't?"

His chin trembled. "You won't ever help me like you do the others. You wouldn't do my chores when I asked you, and you wouldn't play a game with me and you yelled at me."

Libby flushed.

"Is that right?" asked Chuck.

She nodded. "I was thinking too much about the twins. I was scared and I'd hurt my arm and I didn't know what to do." She walked to Toby. "I'm sorry, Toby. I won't yell at you again, and I'll help you when you need help." She remembered the times when she hadn't been able to say she was sorry when she'd wanted to. Jesus was helping her.

"I'm sorry too, Libby." Toby grinned self-consciously. "I didn't really want to get you in trouble."

"Elizabeth, because you couldn't trust enough to share your problems, Toby was hurt. And Toby, because you looked too much at your own hurt, you couldn't look past it and see if Elizabeth was acting the way she was for a reason. We're here to help and love each other. No one is alone. I want you both to remember that." Chuck kissed Toby and told him to get ready for bed.

Libby touched Toby's arm and smiled at him. "Good night, Toby."

"Good night, Libby." He returned her smile.

Chuck tugged Libby's hair affectionately. "Let's get out of here so Toby can get to bed."

She walked with him down the hall to the stairs. What would Dad say to her when they were alone? He wouldn't break his word and force the twins to leave tonight, would he? He wouldn't call Mr. Cinder and tell him to come and pick all of them up—including her— would he?

A Talk
in the Study

LIBBY sank wearily to the sofa in the study as she waited for Chuck. It seemed later than nine o'clock. She watched the door for Chuck. He'd gone to the kitchen to tell Susan and May good night. Was he secretly telling Vera that the first thing tomorrow the girl they'd prayed into their family would have to go?

Libby moaned and curled up in a corner of the couch, protecting her sore arm. Her dream was dead. She might as well get used to it. Why try to fool herself any longer? This whole life with the Johnsons, this whole way of living, was a fake. God didn't love her. She wasn't important to him at all.

Tears stung her eyes and she defiantly brushed them away. When Chuck came into the study, Libby glared at him, defying him to fool her a minute longer. She wasn't fooled. Nobody loved her and no one ever had!

"I can see by your face that we have some talking to do," said Chuck, standing in front of her.

She leaped up, protesting. "We don't have anything to talk about! Go right ahead and make me leave here. See if I care!"

"Elizabeth." His voice was soft and gentle and tugged at her heart. "Satan is a deceiver. He wants you to think bad thoughts about this family—that we don't care for you, that you're not wanted or loved. Just yesterday we read the Scripture that said we are to put down all vain imaginings and trust only in what God's Word says about things."

He sat down next to Libby on the sofa and caught her hand. Then he slipped his arm around her and pulled her close, so their heads were touching. "You belong to this family, Elizabeth. This family belongs to you. God gave us to each other. We prayed you here and here you'll stay. God loves you. I love you. We all love you."

The words melted the ice that seemed to be around her heart, and she soaked up his warm, gentle hug. How many times would

Dad have to reassure her before she believed him?

"Elizabeth, your problems are our problems. You can trust us. You can trust me." He held her away and looked down into her face. "You've been worrying yourself sick because of April and May. I would have helped them, honey. Vera would have helped them. You are not alone! Please, please remember that."

"I'll try, Dad. I'm so glad you don't hate me."

He tapped the end of her nose. "I love you. No matter what you do, my feelings will not change. I love you with God's love, honey. Because of that, my love doesn't change because one day you're good and one day you're bad. And neither does God's love for us. His love never changes. We must learn to love everyone with God's love."

She tried to understand what he was saying, but it was hard. In all her years she had never been loved. There were times when someone liked her for a while, but then hated her when she got mad at the person or did something mean. She didn't know what to say to Chuck. What did he want her to say?

He smiled and leaned against the back of the couch, with his arm still around Libby.

"Can you tell me why the twins ran away from the family they were with?"

She stiffened and she knew he felt it. "They want a family who loves them."

Chuck was quiet for a while and she could hear his heart beating. "Did you ever live with that family?"

She squeezed her eyes shut tightly. "Yes," she whispered.

"And did you run away?"

"Miss Miller came and got me after I called her."

"Why didn't you want to stay?"

Libby jerked away from him and jumped up, her chest rising and falling as she tried to take in breath. "I don't remember!"

He caught her hand. "Yes you do, Elizabeth."

She shook her head hard. Her mouth was cotton dry. "No. No!"

"All right. All right, Elizabeth." He stood up and rested his hands on her shoulders. "I won't ask you again tonight. Just remember what I've told you before." He tipped her chin up until she finally looked into his hazel eyes. "You can give those bad memories to Jesus to heal. Never stuff the memories deep inside yourself and lock the door on them.

When you remember something that hurts you, ask Jesus to heal the pain it brought you then and now."

"It . . . it hurts too much to even remember," Libby whispered hoarsely.

"No matter how much it hurts, it's better to let it out. Once Jesus takes care of it, it won't hurt you again."

"I won't remember, Dad. Don't make me."

He pulled her close and held her. She could smell his aftershave lotion. "Honey, I won't make you. Just remember that God knows everything about you already. He knows what's bringing you pain. He wants to take care of it, but he can't until you give it to him."

She slipped her arms around his waist and hugged him tight; then she cried out in pain. "Oh, my arm!" She held it in front of her and rubbed it.

Chuck gently took it between his large hands. "Tonight we prayed for Jesus to heal April of her cold. We will do the same for your arm." He carefully touched the bruised area while he prayed. "Father, please take care of Elizabeth's injured arm. Help the arm to heal quickly so she can use it normally. Thank you, Father, that you love us. We trust you always. We love you. In Jesus' name, Amen."

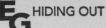

Just then the study door opened and Vera walked in. "Did you call Mr. Cinder yet, Chuck?"

He shook his head. "I'll do it right now. Elizabeth, you sit down again so you can listen to the call. I don't want you going to bed with a single worry on your mind." He smiled as he lifted the receiver to his ear. "Did May get off to bed all right?"

Vera nodded. "I know she'll sleep well after the soup I fed her. She was very hungry. She hadn't wanted to bother anyone for food." Vera sat beside Libby and patted her knee. "I'm glad the twins came to you for help. What if they had gone somewhere where they would have been hurt, or worse?"

Libby smiled, glad that Vera had said that. Then her head snapped around as she heard Chuck explain to Mr. Cinder about having the twins.

"No, I don't want Mrs. Blevins to pick them up tonight," said Chuck firmly. "You know you can trust me, Mr. Cinder. The girls refuse to return to the foster family they were with. I'd like you to investigate that family."

Libby shivered and Vera squeezed her hand.

"Are you sure that they are a good couple

for foster children to live with?" Chuck
frowned as he thoughtfully looked at Libby.
She wanted to scream at Mr. Cinder and tell
him that the Sterns were bad. "I know foster
families are hard to find, Mr. Cinder. I also
know that you want good homes for the children under your care. Mrs. Blevins could be
mistaken about them." He hesitated and
Libby listened intently. "Mr. Cinder, why
don't you leave the girls with us for a few days
until you can check into this? I'll take full
responsibility for them. They won't run away
from us." He listened for a while, then hung
up with a satisfied smile.

Libby leaned back, weak with relief.

"I am believing God for the right family for
the twins," said Vera softly. "God loves April
and May. And I know he has a family for
them."

"I believe that with you," said Chuck.
"How about it, Elizabeth, my girl?"

"I will believe that too," she said with a
smile. She jumped up. "I'm going to tell May
about Mr. Cinder letting them stay awhile.
She'll be happy. I know she will."

"If she's asleep, tell her in the morning,"
said Vera. "Both girls need rest."

Libby kissed them both good night and

hurried upstairs. Just a short time before, she'd felt unhappy about everything. Now she knew everything was going to be just fine.

Susan stopped her outside her bedroom door. "Tell me, Libby. I can't go to sleep until I know!"

Libby laughed softly as they walked into Susan's room and closed the door. "The twins get to stay a few days while Mr. Cinder looks into the home they were in. I know he'll find them a better home."

Susan bounced around on the bed gleefully. "I can't wait to tell the twins."

"Come with me now and we'll tell them." Libby walked down the hall with Susan. "Mom said that if they're asleep not to bother them until morning. Oh, I hope they're awake!"

"Me too." Susan giggled and her blue eyes sparkled with excitement. "I wish the twins could live here always. Then we'd have four girls and three boys."

Libby eased open the guest room door, glad that they didn't have to lock it tonight. She peeked in, then shook her head sadly. "They're sound asleep," she whispered as she pulled the door shut. "I'd like to wake them up and tell them."

"Let's do." Susan reached for the doorknob but Libby stopped her.

"We'll tell them in the morning, Susan." She yawned wide. "I'm going to bed. See you in the morning."

"Good night, Libby. I'm glad you didn't get in trouble with Mom and Dad."

"They love me, Susan," Libby said in awe.

"I know."

Libby flushed and ducked into her room.

Susan poked her head into Libby's still-dark room. "I love you too, Libby. I'm glad you're my sister."

Libby wanted to hug her but she felt too shy. "I love you, Susan." Susan whispered good night again and left. Libby whirled around the room, her arms stretched wide.

Suddenly she stopped and dropped to her knees beside her bed. "Heavenly Father, I'm sorry that I thought you didn't love me. I know you do. I love you and I love this family you gave me. Thank you for helping me and helping the twins."

She prayed quietly for a while longer, then quickly slipped on her nightgown and climbed into bed. She smiled into the darkness. Was this really Elizabeth Gail Dobbs? She felt like a different girl than the one who had moved to the Johnson farm almost a year ago. How different would she be next year?

But what if she wasn't here next year?

Abruptly she pushed the thought aside. She would be! "Thank you, Father, that I will be here next year and the year after that, and I will be more like Jesus all the time."

With a contented smile, Libby turned on her side and closed her eyes. God would help find a home for the twins that was just as great as this home.

"In the morning I'll tell them," Libby whispered as she fell asleep.

April
and May

LIBBY sat up in bed with a start. Rain lashed against her window. The dim light from the hall cast dark shadows in her room. What had made her wake up? She frowned thoughtfully. Then the nightmare rushed back on her, and she moaned in pain, covering her face with her hands.

Why had the nightmare started again? She had pushed Morris Stern to the back of her mind and had refused to think about him for so long now. In her dream, she had run from him, run until she was weak with exhaustion. Then he'd caught her; no matter how hard she tried, she couldn't get away.

A bitter taste filled her mouth as she once again felt his hands all over her. "I won't think about it!" she whispered urgently. "I won't!"

The bed shook with her shivers. Then she began to relax as she forced her mind to think about playing the piano for Rachael Avery. Libby wiped the perspiration off her forehead. She needed a drink of water, so she headed for the bathroom.

After her drink Libby stopped outside the guest room door. Did April or May, especially, ever have nightmares about Morris Stern? Libby rubbed her hands down her flannel nightgown.

Slowly Libby pushed the half-opened door wide and stepped inside the guest room. She would not wait until morning to tell the twins that Chuck would help them and that they could stay here while Mr. Cinder investigated Morris Stern.

Libby walked to the side of the bed, then gaped in dismay. The bed was empty! The twins were gone! Libby's heart sank.

She flicked on the light and looked around the empty room, making sure to look under the bed in case they were hiding. A piece of paper on the nightstand caught her eye. She picked it up and read: "Libby, thanks for helping us. We couldn't wait until morning.

We will not go back to the Sterns." It was signed April and May.

When had they left? How far could they go in the rain? She looked at the clock. It was eleven-thirty. She had thought it was at least three or four in the morning. She hurried breathlessly to her room.

Quickly Libby tore off her nightgown and slipped on jeans and a sweatshirt. Where should she look first? Had they gone down the road hoping to hitch a ride? Oh, why hadn't she told them the good news before she'd gone to bed? It would have been better to wake them and tell them.

She rushed downstairs, then stopped abruptly, her hand on the newel post, remembering what Dad often said: She should not solve her problems alone when he'd gladly help her. Should she call him? Was he already asleep? The rain was loud against the house. The twins were out in that right this minute. Dad might be able to find them faster than she could.

Libby ran to Chuck and Vera's bedroom. She peeked in nervously. She could tell by the steady breathing that they were asleep. Should she wake Dad? Oh, she had to! She touched his arm.

He jerked awake. "Who is it?" he asked sleepily.

"Me. Libby."

He sat up. "What's wrong?"

"The twins are gone."

He immediately reached for his jeans on a chair next to the bed. "Wait for me in the hall. I'll be right out."

Libby practically ran from the room, anxious to start looking for the girls.

Moments later, Chuck hurried out of the bedroom, tugging a sweatshirt over his head. "Are they out of the house?"

"I only looked in the spare room, but they left a note saying that they couldn't wait until morning. They won't go back to the Sterns."

"Elizabeth, why won't you tell me about that man? I have all kinds of wild ideas, but I need to know the truth about him so I can really help the girls."

Her eyes widened in fear and she backed away, bumping into the wall. "I can't tell!"

He studied her face, then slowly shook his head. "I won't make you. Let's find the girls." He led the way to the back porch. "Elizabeth, God knows right where the twins are. Let's ask him to lead us to them quickly."

Libby nodded, once again thankful that

she'd called Dad to help her. His hand closed around hers, and she bowed her head next to his as he prayed. Would she ever remember to ask God to help her the way Dad and the others did? Usually she remembered only after she was really in trouble. Dad often said that they should depend on God to help them in the first place, *before* the trouble came.

Chuck handed Libby Ben's raincoat. "Slip this on over your jacket. That rain will be cold and uncomfortable."

"I wonder what time the girls left the house," said Libby as she pulled on a wide-brimmed rain hat.

"I checked on them about eleven, so they couldn't have gotten very far. I just wonder if they walked outdoors, then decided to sleep in the barn until the rain lets up."

"Do you think so?" asked Libby excitedly. "We could look in the horse barn where they first hid in the hay."

"Let's go." Chuck smiled as he reached for the doorknob.

The rain whipped against them as they ran to the barn. It sounded extra loud to Libby as it hit against her hat and coat. Without rain gear the twins would be soaked to the skin before they reached the barn.

Libby followed Chuck into the dry barn. When he turned on the light, she blinked against the brightness.

Jack and Morgan moved restlessly in their stalls. Libby remembered when she'd first seen the matched grays. She'd never seen such big horses in all of her life. At first she'd been frightened of them, but when she learned how gentle they were, she had lost her fear.

She could not think about the girls not being in the barn. It would be terrible if they'd already hitched a ride and were long gone.

Chuck touched her arm and motioned toward the hiding place in the hay. The girls were curled up together, sound asleep, their green jackets bright against the dull yellow hay.

Libby gripped her hands together as Chuck bent and gently shook the girls awake. They leaped up in fright. May started crying and April glared first at Libby, then at Chuck.

"We're leaving this place and you can't stop us!" April lifted her chin high, her eyes dark with anger.

"Girls, listen to me," said Chuck firmly. "I talked to Mr. Cinder tonight. He said you could stay here while he checks into Mr.

Stern's actions. He doesn't know what he's looking for, he said, but he'll do what he can."

"And we can stay here?" asked May doubtfully, dabbing at her tears.

"Yes," said Libby. "I told you Dad would take care of things."

April sank onto a bale of hay and covered her face with her hands. May wiped her nose with the back of her hand. "You wouldn't lie to us, would you, Libby?" asked May.

"No." Libby smiled and touched May's arm. "Dad will make sure you get a nice home away from Morris Stern."

"Honest?"

April looked up. "Do you really trust Chuck, Libby?"

Libby looked quickly at Chuck and he smiled reassuringly. "I trust him. He won't let us down."

Chuck cleared his throat. "Not all men are like Morris Stern. You must know that." He took off his hat and shook off the rain. "I think you girls had better get back to the house and into bed. Unless you want to sleep here all night." He laughed and Libby saw his eyes twinkle.

"It's too cold," said April, shivering. But she grinned and there was a sparkle in her eyes.

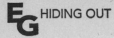

Libby stared at her in surprise. "April! You're better!"

She gasped. "I forgot all about being sick!" She turned to Chuck. "My head doesn't hurt anymore." April put her hand to her forehead. "I don't feel as hot. I *am* better!"

Chuck smiled. "April, Jesus is healing you just like we said he would. Jesus loves you girls. He wants what is best for both of you."

May twisted the toe of one of her soggy tennis shoes in the loose hay. "Me and April once wanted to become Christians. I sure would like to now."

"Me too," said April quietly, tears sparkling in her eyes. "I love Jesus. He helped me get better. He must love me."

"He also helped us find you right away tonight," said Libby.

"Girls, we can pray right now," said Chuck. "Would you like to?"

Libby's eyes filled with tears as the girls nodded.

"In the Bible, Romans 10:9 says that 'if you confess with your mouth that Jesus is Lord and believe in your heart that God raised him from the dead, you will be saved.'" Chuck held his hands out to the twins. They hesitated; then each one reached out and took one

116

of his hands. "Pray with me. Jesus, I want you as my Savior and Lord. Forgive me of my sins and take them away. From this day forward I will live for you, Jesus. You are my Lord. I love you. My life is yours. I belong to you and you belong to me."

As they prayed, Libby remembered the day she'd given herself to Jesus. It had been a wonderful day for her. And she remembered praying with her former enemy Brenda Wilkens when she asked to become a Christian. Now she and Brenda were friends. Libby smiled and wiped tears from her eyes. Now these friends were Christians too.

"Girls," said Chuck with a broad smile for April and May, "this is a very special night for you. You are not alone any longer. Jesus is with you—he will always be with you. Read the Bible to learn more about Jesus. And as you do, you will become more like him. While you are here with us, we'll learn together, along with Elizabeth."

Libby felt like dancing around the barn. What a perfect way to end this day!

"Let's go to the house," said Chuck. "We'll have some hot cocoa before we go to bed."

Libby led the way from the barn, her heart singing with joy.

Morris and Evelyn Stern

LIBBY looked around the classroom. She smiled at Susan, then looked down at her math book. At least she didn't have trouble with math. Susan did, and Libby often helped her.

Libby doodled stars around her paper as she thought about April and May. They'd been at the Johnson farm almost a week. Already they loved and trusted Vera. And they were learning to love and trust Chuck.

What had Mr. Cinder done about Morris Stern? Had Mr. Cinder found a home for the twins yet? Oh, it would be wonderful if they could live with the Johnsons! Adam had been surprised and excited to learn about the twins.

"Libby Dobbs, come to the office," the

voice crackled over the intercom, startling Libby.

"You may be excused, Libby." The math teacher smiled and nodded. Libby tried to walk out of the room without letting everyone know how upset she felt. Her long legs felt like rubbery spaghetti as she walked down the quiet hall toward the office. She pulled her blue sweater tightly around herself and tried to believe that the call to the office was nothing that important.

Miss Richie looked up from behind her desk. "You have a visitor, Libby. He said it was very important to see you. Mr. Page said that you could use his office."

"Thank you." Libby's mouth felt dry as she walked to the small principal's office next to the main office. Her hand trembled as she turned the knob and pushed the door open.

The room seemed to spin as she looked up at the tall, good-looking man dressed in a gray business suit. He smiled but his blue eyes were ice-cold. She tried to leave, but he caught her arm and pulled her into the room, closing the door with an ominous snap.

"I had to talk to you, Libby."

Fear pricked her body as she stared silently

at Morris Stern. His dark hair was combed neatly back from his suntanned face.

"You have nothing to fear from me," he said with a smile. "Shall we sit down and talk? Mr. Page said to take all the time we needed."

Libby's legs gave way, and she dropped to a chair next to the small steel desk. She watched as Morris Stern sat in a chair across from her so that he could observe her face. She rubbed her corduroy pants, then pulled her sweater protectively around her. Why didn't someone come in and rescue her?

"Mr. Cinder talked to me a few days ago. He has the impression that I'm an unfit foster parent. I believe that you've been telling stories, Libby. Am I right?" He lifted a well-shaped eyebrow questioningly. "No matter. Mrs. Blevins said that April and May have taken refuge with you and your family. She said she tried to get them back to us, but Mr. Cinder wouldn't allow it."

Libby swallowed hard, and her eyes darted toward the door.

"Don't try it, Libby. I'm much faster than you." He crossed his legs and leaned back, his arms resting on the arms of the chair. "Listen carefully to me, Libby. If you tell anyone about what happened between us, I'll call you a liar. I will make your new family believe whatever I want them to believe. Mrs. Blevins tells me that they're going to adopt you. If you say anything bad about me, I'll make sure they never adopt you. You know they'll believe what I say, Libby. Adults always believe other adults."

Libby tried to cry out, but no sound came from her throat. She could smell Mr. Stern's strong aftershave lotion, and she thought she was going to be sick.

"Do as I say, Libby, and you'll be happy with the Johnsons. But if you say anything against me, you'll be sorry for the rest of your life." He stood up and walked toward her, towering over her. She cringed away from him. "I mean to have the twins stay with me. Nothing you can do will stop me from getting them back in my home."

Libby closed her eyes tightly, but his image remained inside her head.

"Remember my warning, Libby." He rested his hand on her shoulder, and she jerked violently, cracking her elbow against the wall. "You always were a little fighter. But the fight is over and I have won."

She stared at him as he moved to the door and left. The cloying smell of him stayed long after he left. Libby could not force herself to stand and leave.

Mr. Page walked in, then stopped in surprise. "Are you still here? Didn't you hear the bell ring? It's time to go home."

She tried to stand, but fell back into her chair.

"Are you sick or hurt?" Mr. Page asked in concern, hurrying to her side.

"I'm . . . I'm all right." She pushed herself up and forced her legs to support her. She had to get her jacket from her locker and get to the bus before it left without her.

Hurrying students jostled her in the hallway as she practically ran to her locker. Ben stopped her and asked if she was all right. She mumbled that she was, but he walked with her to the bus, then sat with her.

When she shivered, he asked if she was cold; she said she didn't know. She felt Ben's questioning look, but she leaned her head back and closed her eyes. How could she push Morris Stern out of her mind now? Oh, how she hated him!

She could not race up the muddy driveway with the others, but she walked slowly toward the house by herself. A strange car stood in the driveway, and her heart skipped a beat.

How silly! She didn't need to be afraid of every car that parked in their drive.

April met her on the back porch as she hung up her jacket. The house smelled like fresh-baked bread.

"Oh, Libby!" April caught her hand and held it tightly. "They're here—with Chuck and Vera in the study!"

"Who?" whispered Libby.

"Morris and Evelyn Stern. They got here about five minutes before the bus. May's hiding upstairs."

Libby wanted to run upstairs and hide with her. "What are they talking about?" Libby asked.

"I don't know. Chuck shut the study door." April pressed her hands together in front of her. "Libby, will Chuck let them take us?"

"No. He promised."

"Will he keep his promise?"

"Yes, April." Libby walked slowly toward the study. Oh, what were they talking about? Would Morris Stern convince Chuck not to adopt her?

"Your face is white, Libby. You're as scared as we are, aren't you?" April stopped Libby in the family room. "Do you think we'll have to live with them again?"

Libby remembered how sure Morris Stern was that he'd have the girls back with him, but she would not tell that to April. "I wish we could hear what they are talking about."

"I tried to listen through the door, but the kids came in and I ran away from it."

"Let's go listen." Libby tiptoed to the study door and stood, barely breathing. She could hear voices but not make out the words spoken. How she wanted to rush in and demand to know what was happening. Unhappily she led April back to the family room. How could they stand around and wait to know what was being said?

Just then Vera walked from the study. Libby rushed to her side, asking anxiously what the Sterns were saying.

"They want the twins back," said Vera. "But Chuck said no, and they demand to talk to the girls." She turned to April. "Where's May?"

"Upstairs."

"Get her, please. We'll all talk together." Vera waited until April was gone, then turned back to Libby. "I want you to come to the study with the girls. Chuck seems to think all three of you have something important to say."

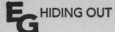

"No." Libby backed away, her eyes wide with fear.

"We'll be right with you. Mr. Cinder said that he would allow Chuck to question the Sterns and the girls, then tell Mr. Cinder his impression of the situation. What Chuck says will help Mr. Cinder decide what to do."

Libby nervously pushed her hair away from her thin face. "Can't he tell Mr. Cinder that the girls can't go back just because they don't want to?"

"It's more than that, Libby. Mr. Cinder wants Chuck to help him find out if Morris Stern's license to have foster children in his home should be taken from him."

"Oh!" Libby's heart leaped in hope. If Morris Stern had his license taken from him, no other foster girl would be in danger from him. Dare she speak up and tell what she knew? But what if he convinced Chuck that she was lying? What should she do?

The twins came down the stairs and stopped in front of Libby. She knew they were as scared as she was. Maybe all three of them together could stop Morris Stern.

Help

LIBBY trembled as she followed the twins and Vera into the study.

Dad told her often that she wasn't alone, that Jesus was always with her. Now, more than ever, she needed God's help and his strength. What she was about to do might stop her from ever being Elizabeth Gail Johnson. And if she wasn't with the Johnson family she would have to give up her dream of being a concert pianist.

She squared her shoulders and lifted her chin high. No matter what happened, she was going to tell just what Morris Stern had done!

Libby felt Morris Stern's eyes on her. She looked right at him, daring him to threaten her again. Evelyn Stern smiled a charming,

easy smile and said hello. Libby managed to speak to her, wondering if she knew what kind of man she was married to.

Chuck sat behind his desk and asked them all to sit down. The twins and Libby sat on the sofa, and Vera sat on a chair beside the Sterns.

"Girls, we're anxious to have you back home where you belong," said Morris Stern with a wide smile that didn't touch his icy blue eyes. "We've missed you."

"We have," said Evelyn Stern in her quick, low voice. "The house is very quiet without you."

"We are not coming back," said April sharply.

"Never!" added May.

Libby saw Evelyn cringe as if she'd been slapped.

"We'll talk about it, girls," said Chuck, leaning forward with his hands clasped together on top of his large oak desk. "May, why don't you want to go back?"

Morris Stern jumped to his feet. "Since when do we ask a child why he or she does or does not want to go home? The girls live with us, and we have every right to take them now."

"Sit down!" commanded Chuck in a voice that Libby knew the man had to obey.

Morris Stern finally sank to his chair, a frown puckering his wide forehead.

"May," said Chuck, smiling encouragingly at her.

May's face flushed red, and she twisted her long fingers together. "Do I have to?"

"Yes, May. You said you don't want to live with the Sterns. We need to know why. Do you want other girls living with them, even though you might not have to?" said Chuck softly.

Libby sat with her back stiff. Could she talk after May told her story?

May's hand trembled as she pushed her long brown hair away from her pale face. Slowly, in a low, tense voice, she told what Morris Stern had done to her, had tried to do to April.

"That's a lie!" cried Evelyn Stern, jumping up. "My husband would not do that!"

"Please sit down," said Vera, catching Evelyn's hand and tugging her down. "Wouldn't you rather know the truth?"

Evelyn sagged into her chair, suddenly looking very old and tired.

"Must we continue with this nonsense?" asked Morris Stern icily.

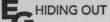

"We must," said Chuck.

May finished her story and everyone was quiet. Libby could barely breathe. Now it would be her turn. She looked at Morris Stern to find him looking at her, defying her to tell what she knew.

"Elizabeth, I hate to make you do something that hurts you, but I want you to tell what you know," said Chuck kindly.

She licked her dry lips and locked her fingers together tightly. May nudged her from one side and April from the other. Taking a deep breath, Libby told her story haltingly. As she told it, the nightmare that was locked inside her seemed to fade away. She heard Vera gasp and Evelyn moan. Finally she finished and Chuck smiled reassuringly at her.

"Mr. Stern, do you have anything to say? I do want you to remember that Mrs. Johnson and I already believe the girls. I already know what I will say to Mr. Cinder."

The handsome man's face sagged. and he slowly stood to his feet in defeat. "At least keep this quiet until my wife and I can move away from this area. It's a terrible story to follow a man around."

"But a true one," said Chuck. "Rest

assured, Mr. Stern, the proper authorities will be notified, and you will never be a foster parent again."

Morris Stern did not answer. He walked from the room, his broad shoulders bent, his head down.

Evelyn Stern slowly stood up, her purse clutched tightly to her. "I didn't know," she whispered, her sad eyes full of tears. "I really didn't know. I'll see that he gets help."

After she left, the room was very quiet. The hall clock bonged five o'clock. Toby shouted something from upstairs. A car drove away from the house.

"It's over, girls," said Chuck.

Libby smiled weakly.

"Now we'll help you twins find a home," said Vera, smiling." Mr. Cinder will allow you to stay with us until a good home opens up."

"Thank you," they said together.

"I'd like to talk to Elizabeth alone for a while," said Chuck. "Do you girls mind going with Vera to fix supper?"

Libby's head felt fuzzy as the twins and Vera left, closing the door behind them. What would Chuck say now? She watched him walk to the sofa and sit beside her.

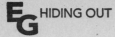

"Honey, thank you for telling that," he said. "It was terrible to have to do, but it's done. But you have one more step in getting rid of it."

"What?" she whispered.

"Jesus will heal the pain that those memories brought you, just as he healed April, and just as he is healing your arm."

She rubbed her arm. "My arm *is* better! It doesn't hurt nearly as much."

"Wonderful! Listen, Elizabeth. Jesus will heal the pain Morris Stern brought you just as he healed your arm."

"How?"

"You have to do something first, honey." He took her hand and held it in his big, warm hand. "The bad feelings you have toward that man have to be released. You must not hate him."

"I hate him!" she cried. "I always will!"

He shook his head. "No. The Bible says that you are to love. You are to forgive."

Libby shook her head hard. "I won't forgive him! He's terrible!"

"Elizabeth, the hurt that he caused you will stay and fester and turn into something terrible if you hang on to it. You must be willing to give up those bad feelings and take Jesus' love and healing. If you do this, you will be able to think about Morris Stern without fear or pain."

"Oh, Dad. I just can't do it."

"Yes you can. We have been learning to live the Bible. We are to be like Jesus. Jesus loves Morris Stern as much as he loves you." Chuck slipped his arm around her shoulder and pulled her close. "You don't have to forgive on your own. Remember how hard it was for you to forgive your real dad for leaving you? Jesus helped you to forgive him. Jesus healed the pain you felt toward your dad. He gave you love for your dad. Jesus will do the same with Morris Stern. Jesus wants you to forgive the man. Jesus wants to heal you inside and take away that hatred."

Libby leaned weakly against Chuck, listening to his heart beating against her ear. "Do I have to, Dad?"

"Do you want to obey the Word of God?"

"Yes."

"Then you have to."

Libby closed her eyes and sighed. "Help me pray, Dad."

As Chuck prayed with her, she felt some of the bitterness and hatred leave. And when Chuck prayed that Morris Stern would find

Christ, she was able to agree in prayer with him.

Finally Chuck held her away from him and looked fondly into Libby's hazel eyes. "You have grown a little more today, Elizabeth."

"I have?"

"Yes. Every time you obey God's Word, you grow spiritually. The stronger you are spiritually, the more you are like Jesus." Chuck stood up and Libby followed him. "It's time we found the rest of the family. They're probably wondering what happened to us."

Libby felt as light as Vera's fresh-baked bread that she could smell in the kitchen. She looked up at Chuck. "I think I'd better practice my piano. I haven't practiced an hour every day the way Rachael Avery wants me to."

"I think you'd better. I'm going to help Ben finish the chores. I asked all of them to do your share."

"Thanks, Dad."

Just as Libby finished the first song on the piano she thought of Toby. He had felt bad a few days ago because she always had others help her or she helped everyone but him. She smiled. He would be gathering the eggs right now. She would help him.

The cool wind blew against her jacket as she ran to the chicken house. Sure enough, she found Toby outside. He looked up with a frown when he saw Libby approach.

"Hi," she said. "I'd like to help you, Toby. If you want, you can go watch TV and I'll finish for you."

He stared at her in disbelief. "What do I have to do for you?"

"Nothing. See my arm? Jesus is healing it. I can use it more now. It still hurts a little, but I just want you to know that I really do love you. I'm glad you're my brother."

Slowly he handed the egg basket to her. "What about April and May?"

"What about them?"

"Are they going to hang around here?"

"For a while."

Toby grinned. "Good. They can learn to do my share of the chores. That will give me more time to watch TV."

Libby laughed. "And do you think Mom and Dad will let you?"

He pushed his hands deep into his pockets and hunched his shoulders. "No, they won't."

Goosy Poosy honked from inside the chicken pen.

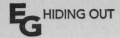

Libby laughed again. "I think Goosy Poosy is agreeing with you. How about doing chores together?"

"All right," Toby grabbed the basket and walked into the chicken house with Libby right behind him. It was warm and smelled bad to Libby. She liked the smell in the barn, but the odor in the chicken house made her sick to her stomach.

Toby knocked a hen off the nest and sent her flying to the floor, squawking noisily. Libby stepped close to Toby, wondering why he wasn't scared of the chickens.

When they had completed the task, they walked into the yard. Toby looked up at Libby. "I'm glad we live with the Johnsons, aren't you?"

Libby nodded. She looked across the yard at the big house, where seven kids lived now, instead of five. "We have the best family in the world, Toby. I know God will find a family for April and May that is almost as nice as ours."

Just then the twins, with Ben, Susan, and Kevin, ran from the barn. Libby watched them come, her heart leaping with love.

Vera opened the back door. "Supper's on, kids. Come and eat."

Libby rushed to the house to have supper with her family, her very own family who loved her.

ABOUT THE AUTHOR

Hilda Stahl was born and raised in the Nebraska sandhills. As a young teen she realized she needed a personal relationship with God, so she accepted Christ into her life. She attended a Bible college, where she met her husband, Norman. They raised their seven children in Michigan, where she lived until her death in 1993.

When Hilda was a young mother with three children, she saw a magazine ad for a correspondence course in writing. She took the test, passed it, and soon fell in love with writing. She wrote whenever she had free time, and she eventually began to sell her work.

The first Elizabeth Gail book, *Mystery at Johnson Farm*, was made into a movie in 1989. It was a real dream come true for Hilda. She wanted her books and their message of God's love and power to reach and help people all over the world. Hilda's writing centered on the truth that, no matter what we may experience or face in life, Christ is always the answer.

Elizabeth Gail Series

1. Elizabeth Gail *Mystery at Johnson Farm*
2. Elizabeth Gail *The Secret Box*
3. Elizabeth Gail *The Disappearance*
4. Elizabeth Gail *The Dangerous Double*
5. Elizabeth Gail *Secret of the Gold Charm*
6. Elizabeth Gail *The Fugitive*
7. Elizabeth Gail *Trouble at Sandhill Ranch*
8. Elizabeth Gail *Mystery of the Hidden Key*
9. Elizabeth Gail *The Uninvited Guests*
10. Elizabeth Gail *The Unexpected Letter*
11. Elizabeth Gail *Hiding Out*
12. Elizabeth Gail *Trouble from the Past*

www.elizabethgail.com

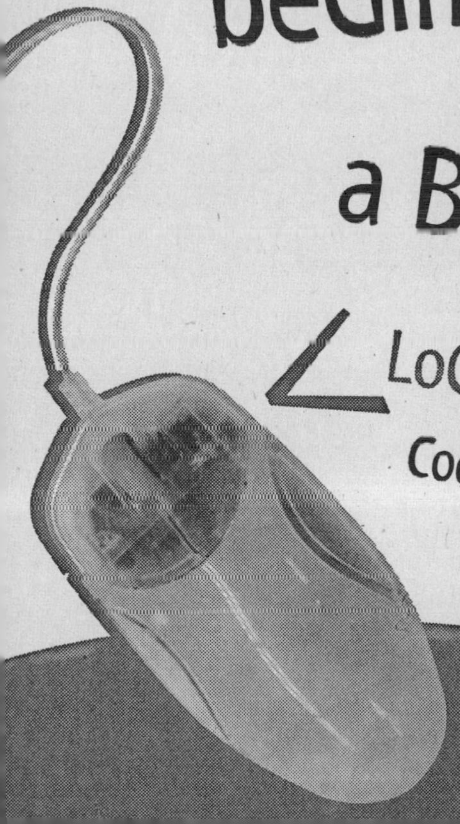